Wayne Collis

They Don't Shoot Cowards

BOOKS BY JOHN REESE

They Don't Shoot Cowards

by John Reese

DOUBLEDAY & COMPANY, INC.

GARDEN CITY, NEW YORK

All the characters in this book
are fictitious, and any resemblance to actual persons, living or dead,
is purely coincidental.

ISBN: 0-385-05577-3
Library of Congress Catalog Card Number 73–79703
Copyright © 1973 by John Reese
All Rights Reserved
Printed in the United States of America

For my grandchildren
KIM, ANDREA, AND CHRISTOPHER
with love

They Don't Shoot Cowards

CHAPTER ONE

They got him between them on the narrow upward trail before he knew what was happening. The older one rode in front. He was a big man, inclined to fat, with a dull slab of a face, one drooping eyelid, and the gray pallor of one coming out of a long drunk. He had a wolf-ish, half-starved look despite his fat. The angular lump in the hip pocket of his Levi's was a .38, beyond doubt.

This one called himself Bud Smith. It was the kind of name you gave the jail deputy when you signed in while you were in no shape to think clearly. "Smith" was unin-spired. The "Bud" probably harked back to the day when he was one of those overgrown bullies who twisted girls' arms on the way home from school.

Bringing up the rear was the kid who called himself Shorty Beaseley, wearing an old .44. He was in his early twenties, a chinless youth with rotting teeth in a gaping, catfish mouth, and scrawny shoulders. To call him a half-wit gave him the benefit of every doubt, but even a half-wit could be deadly with a gun. Shorty Beaseley had the look of a madman with that glittering, deadly skill.

Yes, they had Honker Cahoon in the middle, and he did not like it. He could feel the sweat seeping out of every pore. His very ordinary clothing was worth more than everything Bud Smith and Shorty Beaseley owned.

1

His horse, saddle, and .45 would represent a fortune to them.

"California line's along here somewhere," Bud Smith said, looking back over his shoulder.

"Nobody knows where it is," Honker said in the clanging, braying voice that gave him his nickname. "What do you care? You running for Congress, or what?"

Behind him Shorty giggled his witless giggle. "Can't tell. Bud might settle down and do that, and the Territory of Nevada is no land for a God-fearing man."

Honker did not answer. He did not like that shrill giggle behind him, and that adenoidal grin, but this was not the time to make an issue of anything.

Again Bud looked back. His drooping eyelid gave him the cynical look of a Gila monster with heartburn. "How long was you down there in the Rio valley?" he asked.

"Right at a year," said Honker.

"Yes. Ever run into Lou Burnside down there?"

"Name don't mean nothing. Nobody uses his right name down there."

"Lou Burnside would. Handy as he is with a gun, he wouldn't have no reason to hide who he is."

Honker bayed, "Sure, anybody that makes himself a home-town name by fighting the schoolmarm, he heads for Texas and goes into business as a badman. Brush is full of forty-proof gunnies down there. You flush them out in coveys like quail. About as dangerous too."

Bud scowled and narrowed his one good eye. "I heard there was some real killers down there."

"Only proves you can hear anything."

"If that's how you feel, seems you surely have a reputation of your own. What did you say your name is?"

"I didn't say," Honker snarled.

Bud faced forward quickly, not ready to offend. Honker fought the temptation to wipe his face with his sleeve. It was only August; yet at this altitude the breeze was chilly, and he felt slippery with sweat all over his wiry, warty body.

Two jumps on them was all he needed. Once out of range of the half-wit's .44, his horse would never be caught by their crowbaits. The two jumps were a problem, however. They had left the Nevada desert far behind and were climbing the Sierra foothills steeply. Soon they would be in the tall pines, with no chance to make a run for it even if he could get his lead.

Nothing to do but pretend he was just as vicious as his talk. That took real art, but it was one at which Honker Cahoon had had a lifetime of practice.

In his heart Honker knew he was the worst coward in the world. So far no one had ever found him out. He had led a tormented life, but it had one thing in its favor: it was better than dying. He had hoped to find peace down in the Rio Grande valley, where the runaway riffraff of a hemisphere denned up after making themselves unwelcome everywhere else. Surely, he had thought, these miserable outcasts let one another alone.

That had been the worst mistake of his life, leading to a nightmare year. In his heart Honker was sure most of those half-starved fugitives were cowardly back shooters at best, bluffers who would crawl on their bellies if a real gunman faced them down. The trouble was, how did you tell the bluffers from the real gunmen?

Honker was somewhere in his forties, a supple man of perhaps average height, all gristle, with good shoulders, long arms, and enormous hands. His elemental terror glittered from his eyes with a fire easily mistaken for rage.

They were amber eyes, like a wolf's. His gaunt face was swarthy, Satanic, malevolent. Unfortunately, it was a face no one easily forgot. Across its right side ran a wavering hairline scar that started at the top of his right ear, angled across his temple, and then zigzagged down his cheek to his jaw line. It was the kind of scar that warned men off. One who had survived that frightful wound was bound to be tough, tough!

Honker's drooping black mustache framed a jawful of powerful yellow teeth. His hair was Indian-black but with a tendency to curl when he broke into a sweat, so that he looked like the king of a crew of cutthroat gypsy highwaymen. He wore his .45 in a well-oiled black holster that had been cut away at the top. A leather bootlace held the gun in place when Honker did manual labor.

The bootlace was now untied, leaving the butt of the gun free and fully visible. On its blued forging, between the wooden grips, six beads of gold had been soldered in a row. They could have meant anything, but what they suggested was the equivalent of six notches in a wooden grip. Six golden pips might mean the feats of a killer who was truly dedicated to his art—one to whom each smoking death was a jeweled and unforgettable peak of living.

Honker knew the effect he had on strangers, with his vile eyes, gold-beaded gun, and honking, overbearing voice. And the more frightened he was, the more his voice resembled a coastal foghorn with a sore throat.

At such times the scar on his face turned white, standing out vividly on his dark skin. It enormously magnified the evil of his expression. Scare him enough, and the killer came out—skin-deep, anyway.

A man beholding that white and luminous scar, in one of Honker's fits of terror, might wonder what was left in life for its bearer to fear. So far his mere expression had kept him safe.

Only Honker knew what happened to him inside at the same time. When that white scar jumped out, Honker became stone-deaf. It all went back nearly twenty years, to when Honker was courting a widow woman whose husband had proved up on a quarter section of good Nebraska land before dying with his boots off, of kidney disease. Honker had been helping the widow milk a wild heifer. She kicked her iron hobble loose, and it caught Honker over the ear and cut its way down to his jawbone.

It was the weight of the cow's hoof, on top of the wound, that put him to sleep for fifty hours. He lay there, breathing like a mired mule, his eyes rolled so far back that only the white showed. The doctor said he could not possibly live, and in fact he had dizzy spells for weeks afterward, and suffered from an intermittent deafness that came and went, came and went.

The deafness finally went away, to return only when he was under stress. He fully expected to die in a stone-deaf fit, because he lost control of his treacherous tongue at the same time. When he could not even hear himself talk, how could he know what dangerous things he was saying?

He had run into these two renegades early this morning in the desert. They were badly hung over and had no canteens. Their horses were suffering worse. Honker could not make himself abandon them.

He gave them water from his canteen and led them to a water hole where there was wire grass for the horses. He had no food to share with them, but he boiled the last of his coffee in the can that hung behind his saddle, and what more could a man do than share his last coffee with a stranger in distress?

5

Now they were both recovered from their hangovers but starved to the edge of desperation, and as his horse panted up the trail between them, something like a prayer rose from deep in the yellow interior of Honker:

Don't leave me alone with them, Lord, please. Let somebody come along. Couple of cowboys looking for work. A busted-down prospector. Pair of Washos picking pine nuts. Anybody that will do for witnesses, while I get myself a two-jump head start . . .

Nobody came.

Higher and higher the three riders climbed. Now there were always trees, and the breeze that filtered through the upper passes had the clammy chill of the sea in it. There were creeks and springs. They could have stopped to rest, feed and water their horses, but they kept going. Honker wondered how long it would be before one of their stove-in mounts gave up.

The sun was low over the western peaks when Bud's horse finally quit. Bud lashed it viciously with the split ends of his old reins, but the horse would not move. The big man pulled it crosswise of the trail and looked past Honker to the chinless youth in the rear.

"Hey, Shorty!" he called.

"Yeah, your horse play out?"

"Yes. Know what I wonder? I wonder if our friend here ever run into Pop Watson down there in Texas."

"I bet not," Shorty said, with one of his giggles.

Honker saw Bud's one good eye come into focus on him. "Well, did you?" Bud demanded.

"Did I what?"

"Ever meet Pop Watson?"

"How do I know? I told you, I met a lot of them. Mostly, they're mighty easy to forget."

"Not Pop Watson! He's about the meanest, fastest gunman to come out of Missouri since Jesse James—unless it's his own sons, Merle and Jacob."

"Mean, are they?" Honker yawned. It had a sneer in it, but it was a desperate gasp for breath.

"Yes. Pop wears a long yella chin beard and has got frowsy yella hair, but you'd know him best by his front teeth. They're solid gold."

"Oh, you mean Goldilocks. That's what I called him."

"*What!*"

"This Missourian with the gold teeth. That's what I called him, Goldilocks. Poor, pitiful old codger—he like to fainted, the little run-in that him and me had."

Behind Honker, Shorty Beaseley screeched, "That's a lie! He wouldn't let nobody call him Goldilocks, and he never fainted in his life. That old man is prob'ly the meanest man anywhere in the world!"

"I reckon he whipped the schoolmarm, sure he did. Only way he got out of the third grade prob'ly. If I's getting me up a gang of bandits, he'd be my water boy, and take care of washing the dishes. If I could ever get him over being so scared of me, that is."

Shorty made a strangled, whimpering sound. Bud clamped his mouth shut and stood up in the stirrups. He gave Honker a long, thoughtful, one-eyed stare, and his right hand slid back toward his bulging hip pocket.

"You know what I think?" he said. "I think you're a plumb liar. I'm calling you a liar to your face!"

He went on talking, but Honker Cahoon had gone stone-deaf. He did not even hear his own voice, the sheer, resonating power of which drowned out Bud's.

"You talking to me, you big fat fool? Draw your little old popgun or ride right out of here! I'm losing my patience with you, I do declare. I ought to leave you both afoot on the trail, without your pants on. So this is how you repay a favor, by disrespectful talk. Well, I don't put up with that from nobody, no indeedy. Now get your hand away from that popgun, and tell your half-wit friend behind me to mind his manners likewise, or I'll be forced to draw on the both of you. And I just hate to do that, because already I don't like being knowed as a killer. How would I feel with two more miserable deaths on my reputation, you miserable, ungrateful, lowdown, shote-stealing polecats!"

Bud's slab of a face paled. His hand came swiftly away from his hip. He pushed his old horse down the trail, and Honker made room for him. Bud closed his one good eye and flinched aside as he passed, inches away. He quivered as though feeling the breath of evil on him.

When Bud was out of the way, Honker turned his horse and saw Shorty hesitating with his hand almost on his .44. Honker's smile made that glittering white scar a bloodthirsty battle flag. Shorty changed his mind and led the way back down the mountain, pounding his old horse with his heels every step of the way.

They were a quarter of a mile down the trail before they stopped. They looked back at Honker several times as they talked. Evidently their decision was merely a re-affirmation of their earlier, impromptu ones, because shortly they resumed their descent of the mountain.

A small gray bird cheeped in a pine tree. Two jays coursed down the canyon, shrieking foul names at Honker. A porcupine gnashed his teeth at him, and the thud of a pine cone to the ground resounded echoingly. By these sweet sounds, Honker knew he was still alive.

He had neither died, fainted, nor wept. His scar, his

amber, glaring eyes, his overbearing trumpet of a voice, and his general look of distilled evil had won for him again.

And yet he slumped guiltily in the saddle and faced the fact that he had backslid again. His other vice, as bad as cowardice, was as ingrained in his very flesh—and in the end could be deadlier.

Why, oh why, had he not merely *looked* at them? Men often ran when he did that, with that scar standing out whitely and his eyes glittering. Why could he not keep his big mouth shut?

Besides being the world's worst coward, Honker knew himself to be the world's worst lying braggart. He could not help himself. When he went deaf his tongue took control. In his lucid moments Honker realized that a man who was a coward ought to be a quiet man. If he had to lie, let them be small, harmless lies, like how he once made a hundred dollars a month or was cousin to a congressman. Something like that that wouldn't infuriate anybody.

I wonder, Honker thought, taking his bandanna out to mop his face, who Lou Burnside and Pop Watson are. Nobody I ever met, that's for one hundred per cent sure. And I'll see to it that I never do meet them now. . . .

"Let's go, Horse," he said.

Every mount he had ever owned, Honker had named Horse. This one was a five-year-old brown gelding, tough and willing and fast. Horse was used to Honker's ways by now. He walked carefully until Honker stopped shaking and could be trusted not to fall out of the saddle.

Half-starved, and chilled to the bone, Honker was so glad to be still alive that physical discomfort did not bother him. He rode on until dark.

By then he was high in the "pine zone." He chose a small meadow and staked his mount out with enough rope to get to the clear, cold creek. Horse would dine tonight, but Honker had to pacify his belly with lots of cold water.

He did not fear that those two saddle bums would follow him this high. He built a small fire and sat beside it, wishing he could relax enough to sleep. He looked beseechingly up through the pines at the stars, his amber eyes full of shame and grief. To all men come moments of soul sickness, when life is not worth living and the world is a trash heap and one's own self stands nakedly one's enemy. Such a moment was this for Honker Cahoon.

Why do I do it? Why the *hell* do I do it?

I'll get myself killed with my big mouth.

When I get too nervous, words are like whisky to a drunk. The first one may be harmless, only it leads to another one, and then another one, and so on.

I wish I could go to sleep and never wake up again. Never was good at anything. No good nohow. Just riding from job to job, getting old. No family, no friends. And don't deserve none.

(Honker had two hundred dollars in gold hidden in slits in the two-ply tops of his boots, representing a lucky evening at roulette in Matamoros, Mexico. It was the most money he had ever had at one time in his whole life. He forgot about it as he reproached himself.)

I ort to be content with what I am—nobody!—and yet somebody push me into a fight—oh, dear. Every gunnie anybody ever heard of, I'm the man that made them back down and beg me for their lives. In a pig's eye! Yet it all sounds so real while I'm lying that way. I can see it just as clear, how it happened. Only it never did.

Someday I'll brag to the wrong man. He'll make me pull my gun, and I'll be dead. I'll be—

"Hey, mister!"

It was a soft but shrill voice from the darkness under the trees. Honker went stone-deaf as he threw himself flat on the ground and began rolling down the slope. By the time he came to a stop, thirty feet from the fire, he had the gold-beaded .45 grasped firmly in his hand.

The drumming of his heart told him that his hearing had returned, but there was nothing to hear. On the whole mountainside, there was only silence.

CHAPTER TWO

All Honker could think of was those two saddle bums that had got him between them today—the ones he had got rid of, finally, at no small risk to his life. How they could have caught up with him, on their horses, he could not imagine. But who else could it be?

He lay in silence, clutching his .45, until he had time to think second thoughts. The voice had not sounded like either of those two scalawags, nor was it very likely that they would have hailed him. Rather, they would have been far more likely to cut him down from behind, with both guns and without a word.

Somehow he got up nerve enough to squeak, "Who's that?" In any other man, that is, it would have been a squeak. In his voice it came out a nervous rumble.

No answer. "I said who's that hiding in the dad-blamed darkness like a dad-blamed back shooter? Come out in the firelight and let me see you."

There was a rattle of brush, and a figure came into the circle of firelight—a gaunt, gangling kid who could not be more than eighteen—nineteen at the most. He was nearly six feet tall, but if he weighed a hundred and thirty, he had his pockets full of rocks. He carried a lever-action .30-30 carbine in both hands.

"Gee whiz, you sure are spooky!" he said in a shrill,

boyish voice. "I only wanted to ask you if I could warm up at your fire."

"That carbine the only gun you got on you?"

"Any fool could see that!"

"Maybe I ain't a fool and have to be told. Anybody with you?"

"No. I'm plumb alone."

"Who are you? What's your name?"

The youth gulped. "J—J—Johnny Smith."

"You lie in your teeth! Why can't you kids ever think up some new names for a change when you fight with the schoolmarm and run away from home?"

Honker stood up and came toward the kid, carrying his .45 in his hand. "Mister," the kid said, "I swear that's the truth. My name is Smith."

"Sure, and mine is George Washington. You're a disgrace to your family, whoever they are. When did you have a bath last, or wash your clothes?"

The boy's shirt was old, worn, and filthy. His pants had been cut down from a grown man's. His uncut pale-brown hair stuck through the holes in his dirty old rat's-nest of a hat. His boots were somebody's castaways from a long time ago. The heels were so run over it was hard to suspect them of having any soles at all.

"So your name is Johnny Smith," Honker said in the tones of a hanging judge.

"Yes sir," the boy replied.

"No it ain't. I'll tell you what your name is, since you choose to lie to me. It's Beanpole. No, that's too polite for you. Your name is Beansie, you got that?"

"If you say so."

"How old are you, Beansie?"

"Twenty-one."

14

"That's your second lie. Eighteen is more like it. What are you doing afoot in the mountains with your daddy's saddle gun?"

"I ain't afoot. I tied my horse down there a piece the minute I seen your fire. I—"

"Why'd you do that?"

"It's a good horse. If you turned out to be an outlaw or something, I didn't want my horse stole."

"When did you eat last?"

The kid said eagerly, "Yesterday sometime, but I got a spring deer I shot this afternoon. If you fancy some fresh deer meat, sir, we could cook it at your fire."

"Why didn't you cook it before this if you shot it this afternoon?"

"I haven't got no matches, sir. I got mine wet a couple of days ago."

Surely here's somebody worse off than I am, Honker thought. And he's right: he's got meat and I got a fire, and he's cold and I'm hungry. That's how partners are made, sometimes. . . .

"Don't you even want to know my name, Beansie?"

"Well—yes sir, if you don't mind."

"It's Wilber W. Cahoon. My friends call me Honker, but I'm Mister to you, at your age. I notice you say 'sir' too. That's a good habit to keep up."

"Yes sir. Can I ask you a question?"

"Yes. I might even answer it."

"What's them gold studs on your gun for—the men you killed? Gee! I never knowed a real gunnie before, but I look up to a fast-draw artist more than anybody."

"You unmannerly brat, you ort to have a whipping, to ask a stranger a question like that."

"Heck, I didn't mean no harm. Say, wouldn't it be

15

something if you turned out to be a famous gunman?"

"It sure would," Honker said. "Let's go get that deer of yours and your horse."

They started down the trail together. "All right," Beansie said, "but you didn't tell me what them gold studs are for."

"That's right, I didn't, did I?" Honker snarled.

The kid took the hint. They found where he had tied his horse to a low tree limb, and led it back up to the fire. The kid had no stakerope, but he said the horse would not stray far from Honker's.

The deer was young and fat. Honker took care of the meat while the boy rustled firewood in the dark. First, Honker cut a dozen switches from the nearby brush, which he sharpened at both ends. He stuck them into the ground so they leaned toward the fire. He skinned out a hind quarter of the deer and sliced long, thin slivers of meat, which he impaled on the switches.

The meat broiled quickly, and soon they were eating as fast as Honker could slice it. Honker was prepared for the mellow feeling of well-being that came with a contented stomach. It was something a man had to guard against, to stay out of trouble. Many a man went soft in the heart at the wrong time and later regretted it.

Time to put this dirty, ragged kid in his place. "Where'd you come from, Beansie?"

"Yander." The boy waved his arm.

"Yander. I see. Well, the Mississippi River is yander, and then the Atlantic Ocean, and then England and so forth. What I had in mind, Beansie, was where you started this trip from."

"I ain't going to tell you that, sir, but it don't make no difference, because I ain't never going back there."

"Let's try it another way. Where you headed for?"

"I don't mind telling that. Camp Corinth, in the Sierra Nevada."

"I been all over the Sierra Nevada, and I never heard of no Camp Corinth."

"It's on Fat Tree Creek, I'm told, just above where it flows into the Mokelumne."

Honker exploded. "That rips the rag off of my sore toe for sure! Listen—ten years ago I wasted a whole summer prospecting for gold along Fat Tree Creek. There ain't no Camp Corinth anywheres near there."

"It's a new town, sir. They got a mining boom on."

"If there was any gold in that creek sand, I'd've found it, kid."

"This is silver, sir, and it's hard-rock ore in the canyon wall. Some eastern outfit bought up all the claims at a place they call Stairsteps. They say they're paying tunnel muckers two dollars a day. Did you ever hear of Stairsteps? What's a tunnel mucker, sir? Do you really believe anybody would pay two dollars a day?"

Honker covered his eyes with his hands and moaned deep in his throat. "Stairsteps is where I camped all that summer, wearing my clothes out looking for placer gold in the creek. Canyon wall breaks off there, so it really does look like a stairsteps, but who'd think to look for silver in it? Are you funning me, Beansie?"

"No sir. I hear them Stairsteps claims sold for twenty-five and thirty thousand dollars apiece."

Honker uncovered his face. His eyes were bleak and hopeless, his mouth downcast. "Used to leave my camp before daylight every morning, to make it to the creek in time to get in a full day's work. No wonder I never found silver there. I never seen it in the light. The kind of luck

I have, Beansie—if it started raining diamonds all over a crowd of ten thousand, I'd be the only man in it struck dead by lightning."

"It's hard lines, sir. What's a tunnel mucker?"

"I hope you never find out. You break and load forty ton of hard-rock ore a day. It's a job for a strong back and a weak mind, and your back ain't up to it even if your mind is. Beansie, the only way you can come out ahead on tunnel mucking is to get killed early."

"Well gee whiz though, two bucks a day—!"

"Even if you could get the job—which you can't—you haven't got the heft of it. Ever swing a twelve-pound wedge-hammer all day? I have."

"Heck, I don't know what to do. I got to find me a job somewhere," Beansie said.

He looked so woebegone that Honker took pity on him. He picked up a sharp stick and sketched a map in the dirt beside the fire.

"Look, Beansie—here's the Mokelumne, and here's the ford across it. Now here to the northwest is where Fat Tree Creek flows in, right down this canyon. Now you turn east, there's about a thousand-foot ridge, and then you drop down into a little valley. There's a man there that runs a couple of thousand cows, and he pays a winter man sixty dollars a month. I worked for him one winter. I think maybe I can get you a job there, too."

Beansie sat with his knees drawn up, his arms across them, and his chin dejectedly sunk on his hands. He shook his head slowly. "It'd be too fur from Camp Corinth, sir. It ain't just a job I want. I want to get rich."

Honker shook his head hopelessly. "You want to get rich—I see. Too good to work for sixty a month."

"No sir, but—"

"Beansie, I been making my way in the world since I was twelve years old. Everybody in a mining camp is there to get rich—and I know, because I seen a few of them. But the way it generally works out, one or two men get rich and the others just get old."

"Them that hit silver and sold out their claims, they got enough to be called rich," Beansie said stubbornly.

"And I bet they already lost it. What do they know about handling money? What do *you* know about it?"

"Well, what do *you* know, sir?"

"Nothing! That's why I'm a poor man. You can ride with me if you like, and we'll take a look at Camp Corinth. But then *I'm* going over and get me a job with Bill Shenker, that owns the Zigzag T, and *you* can stay there and get rich if you like."

Beansie hurled a stick into the fire with such force that a shower of sparks flew up. "I don't aim to be a cow hand all my life!" he said.

"Then what do you want out of life?"

"I want people to look up when I ride into town. I want them to know me the minute they see me. I want them to walk safe and soft around me, and after I'm gone, never forget how close they was to me. Only two ways a man can do that—be a fast-draw artist or get rich."

Honker could suddenly remember dreaming the same fantastic dreams at the same age. And oh, how long ago it seemed. More than one lifetime, really.

Honker came from Kentucky. He had not known his parents—and could not forget the uncle who took him in at their death. Uncle Vidal was the only Unionist in a slavery town at a time when neighbor hated neighbor and kin fought kin over abolition.

Uncle Vidal hated slavery because a slave cost money,

and an orphan nephew was free. Honker ran off when he was twelve. By the time he was eighteen he was standing off Indians and rustlers for a cow outfit at ten dollars a month. Later, lumber camps for a dollar a day, and grading camps for a quarter more, looking a four-mule team in the rumps from sunup to dark and taking care of the mules on his own time. Three trail drives up from Texas, and he was broke the day after they hit Dodge City.

All this the kid still had to experience and learn and, if he was lucky, survive. It was an awful thing to be young, and lucky the young did not know how awful it was.

"Here's plenty more meat, Beansie," Honker said.

"I ain't hungry."

"You'll be tomorrow. When you work for a living you got to eat like a boy-constructus snake. Fill your gut while you can, because there's a hungry day coming sure."

Beansie came to the fire for a slice of meat but immediately went back to his .30-30 in the shadows. "I was just thinking, Mr. Cahoon," he said with his mouth full of meat, "what if them two fellas that got you between them today—what if they showed up about now?"

"How'd you know about them two?"

"I seen you. When they got you between them I was sure you was as good as a dead man."

"Them two egg-sucking garden robbers?" Honker scoffed. "Beansie, when you're my age you'll be able to tell riffraff like that when you see them."

"I met a man once claimed he'd seen Dewey Score, but I never met no gun fighter myself," Beansie said.

"You mean the Dewey Score that shot Ontario Slim's ear off after Slim killed King High McKelvey?"

"Yes. You ever happen to see Dewey Score? He was my hero, sir."

Something—jealousy, probably—eased its way into Honker's lonely, humble, cowardly soul like a mushroom bullet and expanded there, pushing out the last of his good sense. Suddenly his ears rang with the memory of shots he had never fired, against gunmen he had never met, in fights he had never fought.

"Do I know Dewey Score?" he said, stretching out full length so he could rest on one elbow. "I'll tell you the truth about that whole thing, Beansie. This fella McKelvey never claimed to be no gunman. He lost his temper one day in a poker game when he stood fast on a pat jack-high straight, and this other fella drawed four cards. Well, it turned out this other fella had a nine-high club flush, see.

"Nobody is going to draw to one little old club in an honest deal and then catch four to go with it. So when McKelvey called him a name, this gambler goes for his gun, and another club fell out of his sleeve. It kind of broke his nerve, you might say, because McKelvey beat him to the draw. He shot him and then said, 'A king-high straight will beat a crooked flush every time, and this here gun of mine is my king.' So that's how he got the name of King High, from this gun of his.

"Ontario Slim come from little old town up in Canada, and he thought he was some punkins of a gunman. He killed King High McKelvey in Pocatello, Idaho, over some quarrel or other, and he really did think he was the world's greatest then. He joined up with Dewey Score's gang of stage robbers and was going to take the gang away from Dewey so it would be called the Ontario Slim gang instead.

21

"But when the two of them had it out, Dewey Score just whanged one of Ontario Slim's ears off, as clean as if the doctor did it with his razor. The thing about Dewey Score—he was a *good* shot, all right, but he was a *lucky* shot too. He was trying to shoot Ontario Slim between the eyes, and he come that close to missing, and yet when he took that ear off, he took the heart out of Ontario Slim."

"Yay!" Beansie breathed. "I sure would like to've seen that gun fight. I reckon Dewey Score was about the best fast-draw artist that ever drawed his gun."

Honker patted back a yawn. "Dewey was a fair shooting man, but I couldn't really respect him. When him and me fell out in Phoenix, Arizona—"

"*You* fell out with Dewey Score?"

"Well, it wasn't nothing serious. It prob'ly wouldn't interest you at all, Beansie."

"Gee! Sure it would! Tell me about it."

Honker told him.

Told how he had sent word he'd wait at the blacksmith shop to talk over with Dewey which one of them was to get a bartending job both of them wanted. Leaned in the door of the shop, ankles crossed, toothpick in his mouth, scratching between his shoulder blades on the side of the door. Waited a good hour and a half.

Finally here came the famous Dewey Score, said to be the fastest man in the world with a gun. He stopped across the street and hollered:

"You want to talk to me, Cahoon—I'll tell you what kind of a talk it'll be. You get five minutes to saddle up and get out of town, or the next talk we have will be with our shooting tools."

To which Honker replied, "If you'd take more time

parting your hair, Dewey, you wouldn't look so bad. It's just the way you comb your hair that makes you look tough."

"No personal remarks!" Dewey screeched. "Draw your gun, draw your gun, draw your gun!"

"My back itches," Honker replied, shifting the toothpick in his mouth. "You draw your'n while I give my back a good scratch. Ah, that just feels wonderful."

Dewey kind of hunched his shoulders down and began shambling across the street, yelling, "Draw, draw, draw!"

"You better not come no closer, Dewey," Honker said. "Not without a gun in your hand."

Dewey stopped and snapped his fingers angrily. "You're just trying to bait me into drawing so you can kill me," he said. "An old experienced gunman like you, it wouldn't bother you none to shoot me, would it? Well, you ain't getting away with it! I tell you fair and square, I'm leaving this town behind, and if you draw a gun on me, it'll be plain premeditated, cold-blooded, first-degree murder."

Honker spat into the fire and watched the sizzle become a black spot, then start burning again. This, he decided, had been one of his best. That part about scratching his back made it seem so real.

And things often happened that way—although not to Honker Cahoon. There *were* men who could pull a gun with the streaky speed of a snake. Many of them *did* become vain about it, and envious of the reputation of others. Now and then two such celebrated artists *did* shoot it out, for no other reason than to settle the debate over who was fastest. And often nerve counted as much as physical speed.

Honker had seen many such noted gunmen—usually, it should be recorded, from the safest distance possible. He had long been convinced that your brittle-tempered, proud, and bellicose speed artist was, usually, too lazy to hold a job at any ordinary kind of work. Hard work meant callused hands with cramps in them, and there went the dexterity by which the fast-draw man survived. But so far it was no more than a theory with Honker. He had no intention of getting close enough to any gunman to test it.

"Gee!" Beansie breathed. "Just think of that. The famous Dewey Score backed down to you. He was always one of my heroes, but he sure ain't no more."

"He wasn't no hero, Beansie. He was just a old dirty-neck cowboy that didn't like the work, so he went around starting fights with people that was scared of him."

"You sure wasn't scared of him. I reckon you must be about the fastest gunman in the whole natural world."

Honker patted his mustache modestly. "Well, all it really takes is plenty of practice."

"And nerve!"

"Not really, kid. What nerve does it take when you know you're the fastest man and the best shot?"

"I reckon that's right. Gee, when you let two of them get you between them, like you did today, and run them off with their tails between their legs—well, nobody but you could've done that. That's not nerve, Mr. Cahoon. That's pure cold faith, sir."

"That trash today? Pshaw, boy—they wouldn't scare a flea."

"Maybe to you, sir, but Lou Burnside is one of the

24

fastest fast-draw artists in the world, and they say Merle
Watson is even meaner and faster than Pop. Yet there
you was, with Burnside in front of you and Merle Watson
behind you. And just when I thought you was as good
as dead, off they go down the trail like a couple of sheep."

"Why, them two riffraff saddle bums—"

Honker suddenly choked up, remembering certain
parts of his conversation with the two on the trail. But
Beansie was going on reverently: "I seen their pictures
in a sheriff's office once, so you bet I didn't let them see
me today. It sure is an honor to set by the fire of the most
dangerous man in the world, Mr. Cahoon. I only wish I
could tell you how much I admire you, sir."

Honker could only wish that lightning would strike
him mercifully dead, or that one of those earthquakes
would crack beneath them and part the mountain to
swallow him up. Those two had only been baiting him
into drawing, and like the big-mouthed, windy fool he
was, he had bluffed them into quitting without even
knowing who they were.

Yet, hurt a gunman's pride, and he'd spend the rest of
his life getting even with you. His reputation was all he
had, as a rule. Reputation saved him many a showdown
fight. Reputation fed him when he was hungry, gave him
whisky when he was dry. Whole towns kowtowed, law-
men found official business at the other end of the county,
and dread slithered ahead of him like a snake, when a
man with a killer's reputation came on the scene.

Lou Burnside and Merle Watson would come after
him once they took time to think it over. They simply
could not afford to do anything else.

"I guess they knowed you by the gold beads on your

gun," Beansie was saying. "I never heard of you, I'm ashamed to say, but they sure did. They—"

"Oh, shut up and go to sleep! We got a long old ride ahead of us tomorrow," Honker snarled.

Beansie lay down beside his .30-30 and was instantly asleep. Honker lay down but not to sleep. It came to him that Burnside and Watson (alias Smith and Beaseley!) could steal two good horses somewhere and be on his tail any time now. He let the fire down and sat wide awake most of the night.

Nobody came.

But Honker did a lot of thinking—the kind of cold, clear-eyed thinking he had never done before. The kid was right: only two kinds of people were respected in this world—those who were too dangerous to offend and those who were too rich. That limited the opportunities of a coward. His only hope was to get rich.

There was money to be made in a boom mining camp. The idiot stampeders did not make it, as Honker knew, having been in a few other mining camps. Heretofore he had always been one of the humble losers who handed over all they had to the real money-makers and left town broker than when they rode in.

A spiritual revolution burned through Honker that night as he shivered through his vigilant sentry-go beside the cold ashes of the fire. I'm turning over a new leaf, he swore, again and again. I got to make money—I got to, I got to! Oh, lordie, I'm such a coward, and such a liar! What else can I do but get rich . . . ?

CHAPTER THREE

Shortly after crossing the Mokelumne River, they came to a trail that, since Honker last saw it, had become a wagon road. And soon after that a man came loping his horse down the road toward them. He went on the alert the moment they came in view, opening his jacket to expose a .45 in a low-slung holster and changing the reins to his left hand.

He was a slim, hard-faced man with a well-kept Van Dyke beard and a neat brown mustache. He pulled up and saluted them watchfully. Honker returned the greeting with a curt nod. He did not like meetings with armed and watchful men on any trail and was alert enough himself.

"Mokelumne ford still open?" the stranger asked.

"Sure," said Honker. "Almost no water at all in it now. Won't be until the runoff next spring. You a stranger in these parts?"

"More or less."

"Know where Camp Corinth is?"

The stranger began cursing. "I should. Just came from there. Worst hellhole I ever seen in all my born days. I wouldn't even go back to haunt it if I was dead."

He saluted them again and rode on. They followed the rough wagon road, which shortly crossed Fat Tree Creek and turned sharply northward, beside the creek.

Suddenly, as they emerged from the stand of softwood timber along the creek and came out on a sloping mountain meadow, the town of Camp Corinth burst upon them.

"I wouldn't believe it if I hadn't saw it myself. Take a good look, Beansie. You never again will see so many fools gathered in one spot," said Honker.

Nothing was familiar to him except the misshapen cottonwood that gave the creek its name. Every other tree along the creek had been cut down. The meadow between the creek and the canyon wall had once been almost a mile wide here. Beyond it was Stairsteps, the three-tiered cliff where Honker had once, ten years ago, camped while prospecting for gold.

Now a continuous cloud of dust, and a continuous thump and rumble, arose from the stamping mills near Stairsteps. Camp Corinth itself, however, had been laid out no more than two hundred yards up the slope from the creek, to make a shorter haul for drinking, cooking, and washing water. It was mostly a tent city—a long, straggling double row of tents and canvas shelters of every description lining both sides of a "street" of mud. A few pole lean-to shelters, roofed with brush, had started to appear, giving the camp a fictitious air of permanence.

It was almost dark, and lanterns had been lighted along the entire street, which was nearly a mile long. It looked to Beansie as though more than five thousand men were milling about in the street, slogging through the mud, going in and out of the tents, and yelling at the tops of their voices.

"Criminy! It's like kicking over an anthill, Mr. Cahoon, ain't it? Are all of them fellas silver miners?" the kid said.

"About one out of twenty. The others only wish they

was. Come on, let's take a look at it, and then I'm going over and hit Bill Shenker up for a winter job on the Zigzag T. You can stay here and get your fool's citizenship papers if you like," Honker growled. "Come on, Horse!"

If there were five thousand men here, there must be five hundred million mosquitoes, it seemed to Beansie. As they neared the closest tent, a man stumbled down the middle of the street toward them, ankle-deep in mud. He had on the remnants of a gray suit and a ruffled white shirt. His white hair hung down over his ears, under his black hat. On his big beak of a nose rose a pair of rimless eyeglasses, with a black ribbon that led to his lapel.

"Welcome, strangers, to the liveliest new city in the history of mankind," he said. "Whether it's town lots or mining properties, I'm the man to see. There is still a lot of rich, ore-bearing land available, and as for lots—"

Honker cut in. "Hidy, Perfessor! You haven't changed a bit in ten years, you old scamp. Meet my trail pardner, Beansie. Beansie, this is Judson Blythe, the best-educated drunk west of the Continental Divide. Most people call him Perfessor."

Perfessor aimed the glasses at Honker, frowning. "Ten years ago? That would be the winter I worked for the Zigzag T as a cowboy."

"That would be the winter you stayed sober because we was all snowed in," said Honker, "but you was still a complete stranger to work when spring came."

"Honker Cahoon, that's who you are! I'd know that voice anywhere. I'm wasting my time on you. The lower classes are becoming impossible," Blythe said with dignity.

He turned and reeled down the street, keeping his feet with difficulty although the glasses remained firmly poised on his nose. Honker walked Horse slowly, Beansie trailing behind him. By the light of the dying day, as well as by the lanterns, they studied the crude signs that hung before the larger tents:

MOM RILEY'S CAFE—ALL MEALS $3 *Haircuts $5—Beards Clipped $2.50—No Shaves* TEETH PULLED, LEAKY POTS MENDED, GUNS REPAIRED, BOILS LANCED *Prof. Godoy, Artistic Tattooing* YUK CHOW, TAILOR, LAUNDRY & MENDING *Dr. Z. F. Olferino, Fortunes Told, Your Stars Scientifically Analyzed.*

There was a brand-new Wells Fargo office but no sign of government—neither sheriff nor constable, neither justice nor judge, neither clerk nor scribe. Just above the tent street, however, on the slope, was a graveyard, obviously growing fast, and another sign over another tent:

UNDERTAKING & BURIAL INSURANCE
Sidney P. Thompson,
Sole Proprietor.
ARTISTIC REDWOOD GRAVE MARKERS!!
Hand Carved—Order Yours Now!

"What's burial insurance?" Beansie asked.

"You pay this fella now, and he guarantees to spade you under respectably if you run out of days," said Honker.

"Does it work?"

"Sure—if somebody don't shoot him before they do you. He don't dare let one of his insurance customers go unplanted. Nothing gives burial insurance such a bad name."

He reined in suddenly before another sign:

WILLIAM SHENKER, MEAT MARKET
Fresh Beef Daily, $2 Lb.

And just beyond the meat market stood the biggest tent of all. It had obviously been made for a circus, since it was of red-and-green-striped canvas. In front of it stood a team of oxen, hitched to an enormous bull-wagon. Four big lanterns illuminated the sign over the double doors of the striped tent:

BILL SHENKER'S SILVERADO CAFE
Drinks $1—All Meals $3
Heavy Hauling—Ask Inside

"If one bait of grub costs three dollars," said Beansie, "how can a tunnel mucker live on two dollars a day?"

"They camp and batch," Honker growled absently.

"I always wanted to get tattooed. How much would it cost to have a red heart tattooed on my arm, with the words 'Annabelle My Beauty' inside, in blue?"

"Is that your girl's name?"

Beansie looked shocked. "Heck, I ain't got no girl."

"Then why do you want 'Annabelle' on your hide?"

"Well, that's my favorite name. If I had a girl, that's what I wish her name would be."

"You really are laying plans to get rich, ain't you?" Honker said. "Not a penny in your pocket, and first thing, you want to get tattooed. Why, boy, inside of a year you'll prob'ly own most of the Union Pacific."

Beansie cringed. "You're right. I'm sorry, Mr. Cahoon. I never will amount to nothing, will I?"

Honker twisted sidewise in the saddle and made himself comfortable. "Don't feel too bad, Beansie. If there's five thousand men here, forty-nine hundred and ninety-nine of them think just like you do. You want to know how to make money here? There!"

He pointed to the two signs advertising the Shenker enterprises, the meat market and the Silverado.

"Bill's got himself a monopoly on the meat trade because he's the only cowman in these mountains. He's a one-man beef trust all by himself, as immoral as a horse-car promoter or a railroad contractor. And there in the Silverado, he's got food, liquor, and gambling—and you don't notice any competition for the rotgut and the games, do you? You mark my words, Beansie; before the ore plays out here, Bill Shenker will own everything. A squirrel is going to have to pay him rent to store nuts in a knothole."

"He won't own all of it," Beansie said grimly. "I'm going to get me some too."

"How?"

"I don't know, but I promise you this: I never will make the mistake again of wanting to be tattooed, or any such fool thing like it, as long as I live."

"It's fine to save, boy, but first you got to lay your hands on something to save."

"I'll figger that out some way. But when I leave this town, Mr. Cahoon, I'll have money in every pocket on me, and people are going to *remember* me. Look at them fools, fighting to get into the Silverado to pay them prices for liquor and food! Why, they ain't no better than a flock of sheep! No sir, you'll never, never, never catch me in no such idiot stampede as that."

Honker's breath came a little shorter, and his heart beat a little faster. All his life he had tried not to attract attention riding into any new town. He was the cheap help, welcome when there was work to be done, but he moved right on when it was over. He had done his share of pushing to get into places like the Silverado and had felt no anger or outrage at getting tossed out bodily when his money was all gone.

Never in his life had he dared to think a thought like the one this long, lean, unripe kid was boldly expressing. Beansie was flighty and mouthy, but he had the right idea, and he was starting young enough to turn dreams into reality.

I'll do it! Honker vowed silently. Turn over a new leaf. No more dad-blamed wasting my life. I may not get rich, but I'll give it the try of my life. . . .

"Come on, Beansie."

"Where to?"

"Wait and see."

"Mr. Cahoon, I'm plumb starved to death."

They had left their camp before daylight this morning, Honker so sure that Lou Burnside and Merle Watson would be on their trail that they had not bothered to cook up the rest of the deer. All they had eaten all day was a few berries snatched from the saddle. Honker was so hungry he was light-headed, too, but he was in the grip of his first attack of towering ambition, and keenly aware that his years were running out. What was mere food beside that?

Or perhaps hunger helped inspire him; perhaps he would not have dared to dream had he not been a little dizzy with hunger. He waited for Beansie to catch up with him and snarled at the boy as they rode.

"We'll eat tonight, don't you worry. But first things first. You hear that critter bawling?"

"What about it? I told you, sir—I don't want no dad-blamed cowboy job."

"Neither do I. Bill Shenker put up a cabin and a corral over here some years back. Was going to winter some cattle here, but the dad-blamed gov'ment run him out. If he's in the meat business, he's got a place to butcher his beef, and I bet I know where it is."

"I don't care where it is. If there's one job I purely hate, it's butchering."

"You listen to me, boy. How'd you like to set down to a big thick steak now?"

"You trying to make me bust down and cry, sir?"

"I'm asking you. Would you give ten dollars for it if you had ten dollars?"

"A hundred. Only you know I ain't got a dime!"

"Yes, but there's thousands of miners here that have to pay whatever Mr. Beef Trust Shenker says, because he's got a filthy dirty miserable money-making monopoly. You seen it yourself. He gets two dollars a pound for beef. *Two dollars a pound!* Suppose your steer dresses out only six hundred pounds, what's it worth in Mr. Beef Trust Greedy Monopolist Shenker's store?"

"That's easy. Twelve hundred dollars, Mr. Cahoon."

"Yes, and I don't begrudge Mr. Beef Trust Monopoly Shenker a cent of it. If I owned live beef, I'd squeeze every last cent I could out of it, myself. But do you know what I think, kid? And you listen and pick your ears clean, because this is the straightest truth in the world."

"All right," Beansie said solemnly.

"Making money is like a disease. It changes you for life."

"That sure is the truth. I never knowed many rich men, but they sure wasn't like common people."

"Now you're catching on. Point is, Beansie, How can you catch the disease unless you're around where it is? We're going to catch it from Bill Shenker. You hear that man hollering? That's him. That's a rich man in distress. You let me do the talking, you hear?"

A light was twinkling through the timber ahead of them. They splashed across Fat Tree Creek, closing in on a protected clearing in the forest. The fire blazed beside a stout log cabin. Behind it was a big log corral.

The gate was open, and a solitary steer was racing back and forth among the trees, pursued by a big, handsome, well-dressed man on a fine horse. Black suit, black hat with silver band, black side whiskers shot with gray, and some handsome gold teeth.

Honker rode out boldly and headed the steer. One "Ha!" from Honker's explosive voice, and the terrified animal bolted into the corral. Honker leaned over and swung the gate shut.

"Howdy, Bill," he said genially. "You never was any good at handling cattle, as I remember, and you ain't a bit better now."

Shenker reined in his horse and glared ferociously at Honker. And for the first time in his life, Honker did not cringe politely. He glared right back.

"Do I know you?" Shenker demanded.

"You should. I worked for you ten years ago this winter. I'm about to go to work for you again, Bill—me and my partner, that is."

"Oh yes, I know that voice. You sound like a bull with his tail caught in the sorghum mill. Let's see—Cahoon, ain't it? You're Honker Cahoon."

"That's me, and this is a poor but honest boy that I've took temporarily to raise, by the name of Beansie. A good boy, and all he needs is training and discipline."

"If he learns anything from you, he's ruined for life. I recollect you well, Honker. You did put in your time here, but you sure never ruptured yourself turning out the work. So don't waste my time, unless you're either a law enforcement man or a beef butcher."

"Why should you want a law enforcement man?"

"The one I had hauled off and quit and run like a cottontail. Real tough man, he used to be, but Camp Corinth took it out of him. Man with a spade beard—"

"I reckon we met him on the trail. I ain't no lawman, Bill, but this is still your lucky day. You just happen to be looking at the two best beef butchers in the whole natural United States."

"You're no beef butcher!"

"I ain't going to argue with you, but I do wonder what you want with a butcher, with only one beef to butcher."

Bill Shenker was close to tears. "There's supposed to be three butchered every day. I had three men, no other job than to run them over from the home place every few days, fifteen at a time, and butcher three for me every day. I should've knowed what would happen when they made me pay them every night. Minute they got a few days' pay, they run off to go prospecting."

"Bill, you heard of opportunity knocking at your door? This time it's smashing your door down with a sledgehammer. Me and Beansie can do your job for you."

Bill narrowed his eyes. "You could do part of it mebbe. Suppose I give you a chance—how long can I depend on you to stay, at three dollars a day?"

Beansie gave a startled, incredulous yelp, but Honker bayed, "About ten minutes, at that price. Make it ten a day, and we'll shake on it."

"Ten dollars a day?" Bill shrieked.

"Plus a full load of groceries so we can do our own cooking and not have to eat in your thieving Silverado.

Plus blankets for the cabin. We get paid every evening, and you stay plumb away from here all day until we tell you to come for your meat. We'll do you a good job, but we don't want nobody hiding behind the trees to see how we do it, and steal our trade secrets."

Shenker choked. "I'll see you in hell first!"

Honker slipped from the saddle and threw the reins over his horse's head. "You might, at that. All right, we'll just water our horses at the creek and go find us something else to do."

"But ten dollars a day!"

Bill's horse went up on its hind feet as Honker turned and said savagely, at the top of his voice, "Let's look this pot over together, you thieving old idiot! A steer dresses out at twelve hundred dollars. Three of them, that's thirty-six hundred dollars. Besides that, you've got the saloon and your gambling. Why, Congress ought to pass a law against you! You're worse than the banking octopus! You're taking in five thousand dollars a day. You think I can't figger? *Five thousand dollars a day!*"

"Sh-h! Sh-h! Shut up! You don't realize what you're saying, Honker. You want to holler that over the *in*tire mountain?" Bill was pleading.

Honker mounted his horse. "Come on, Beansie, let's leave this titan of illegitimate misfinance to his own filthy, dirty, reeking conscience. We don't want to mix with no beef monopolists nohow."

"Five dollars a day," Bill coaxed.

"We'll go into the deer meat business with your thirty-thirty, Beansie," Honker said, turning his back on Shenker. "Five dollars a day—why, what does he think we are, a couple of jobless cowpunchers?"

"You're on my land!" Shenker shouted. "Any deer here belong to me."

"If we shoot any with your brand, we'll split with you." Honker whirled his horse so suddenly that Shenker's went up on its hind feet again. "Bill, you're using up my patience fast. You want this lonesome steer butchered tonight or don't you? Ten dollars a day, payable every night, and groceries and blankets for the cabin."

"You're just a cold-blooded holdup man, but what can I do?" Shenker whimpered. "All right, it's a deal. I'll go fetch my bull wagon to bring the beef back, and I'll bring your groceries at the same time. See you in about an hour and a half."

"And bring our day's pay too. Ten dollars each!"

"A day's pay? Why, you ain't even started to work yet, and here it is night!"

"We'll butcher your one steer for you. It ain't our fault that one is all you've got. Bring our pay with the groceries if you want any meat tonight."

"You are absolutely without mercy, Honker. An old friend like you, I just don't see how you can do this to me," Shenker said sorrowfully.

He put his horse into a run back to Camp Corinth. Honker watched him with a strange expression. "How do do you like them apples," he said.

"I can't believe it!" said Beansie. "Me—getting ten dollars a day. You sure did handle him noble, sir."

Honker shook his head. "You'll look after me, won't you, Beansie, and not let some little girl in a pinafore take everything I own? He'd've went to twenty a day just as easy."

"I reckon so."

"I see now there's more than one rule to making money.

I stood up to him like a mad bull, all right. But I was betting penny chips in a ten-dollar game—and that's a mistake I won't never make again."

Abruptly he rode off through the timber, leaving Beansie standing with his mouth open beside the corral.

CHAPTER FOUR

Beansie stood there only a moment, feeling lost, and more hungry than ever. He had no idea where Honker had gone or when he would be back. He went into the cabin and looked around. There was a lamp on the table, another hanging from a baling wire from the roof. He found matches over the stove and lighted both.

It was a snug, well-made cabin with a plank floor and not small by any means. There were two big comfortable bunks in one end. At the other was a cast-iron stove and a table and chairs. He rummaged through the shelves but could not find a bite of anything to eat.

There was a little wood in the wood box. He started a fire, remembered a woodpile he had seen out back, and went for more wood. When the box was full he used an old broom he found leaning in a corner and swept the plank floor. He filled the water pail and teakettle at the creek.

He heard voices in the timber as he returned to the cabin with the water. He put the teakettle on the stove, stoked the fire again, and went outside. Honker Cahoon was walking his horse through the brush toward the cabin, surrounded by at least twenty Indians of all ages. They were all afoot and all seemed to be enjoying themselves.

"Beansie," Honker said, dismounting, "meet my old friend, Ambrose Green Snake, chief of this family of the

Washo tribe. Ambrose, this is a boy I took to raise, Beansie by name."

Beansie shook hands with the Indian, a powerful-looking man with wrinkles of humor in his face but something wary and proud in his black eyes. "Hidy," the chief said. "By golly, we don't like no friends of Bill Shenker, you can bet, by golly! But by golly, Honker's a friend of ours."

"Ambrose and his people are going to butcher for us, Beansie," Honker explained. "Bill wouldn't want them on the place, and they wouldn't lift a finger to help him. So this is strictly between us."

"You bet, by golly!" said Ambrose Green Snake. "Now you watch how we make meat, Beansie."

The whole family filed into the corral. They did not bother with a rope. They swarmed over the steer like hiving bees, in the dark. It was dead, skinned, split, and swinging from a block and tackle in the tree in a matter of minutes.

"They get the guts and the hide," Honker told Beansie as they watched the Indians at work. "I told them to send somebody over later on if they wanted some sugar and stuff. They'll watch when we get back from the home place with more steers tomorrow, and butcher three of them for us."

"Don't you pay them no money?"

"The guts and the hide is all they want. It's a lot more than they've got now."

"Mr. Cahoon, do you think that's fair?"

"It's fairer than they'd get from Bill Shenker."

"That ain't the point, sir. If they knowed how much Mr. Shenker is paying us—"

"But they don't, and they figger they're lucky to get the guts and the hide."

"I still think it's cheating."

"Boy, do you want to get rich, or don't you? You never heard of no rich man worrying about anybody but himself, did you? If you give them Indians money, all you'll do is spoil them."

But his amber eyes fell, he ran out of words, and when the fresh beef was swung up in the tree, he gruffly called the Indians over and gave them what change he had in his pocket. The Washos straggled off through the timber, homeward bound with their loot.

"You had your way, didn't you?" Honker growled. "You done spoiled a perfectly happy bunch of Indians. What can they buy with money? Only things they don't need and are better off without."

Beansie started to say, "My conscience wouldn't—"

Honker cut in harshly, "What has conscience got to do with it? Do you think Bill Shenker has got one? All my life, I've had a perfectly good conscience. Well, where did it get me? Listen, boy—I'll tell you one thing about rich men. They don't even know what a conscience is. To them, people is just plunder, like trees to cut or cattle to raise or ore to dig out of the ground. Take a good look at me, kid, because from now on, I'm out for the plunder."

Toward the last, he was speaking rapidly, having heard Bill Shenker approaching with his big wagon and ox team. "Open the gate," Shenker called, "so I can back in under the meat with the wagon."

His dark face still flushed, his eyes snapping, Honker said, "Let's don't be in no hurry about loading up that meat. First there's the little matter of ten dollars apiece you owe us."

"You've made a mistake, Honker. I never agreed to pay you no twenty dollars for a few minutes' work."

"We done your butchering, and that's what we agreed to do. Ten dollars apiece, Bill—or we cut the rope and let the varmints have it."

Bill looped his bull rope around the wagon's tie post, leaned his prod pole in the wagon bed, and clambered down the high wheel to the ground. "You must have went clean out of your head, Honker. I might go as high as two dollars apiece, but that's every last cent."

Honker looked back over his shoulder. "You see, Beansie? Just plunder!" To Bill he said, "One minute, and I go get the ax and cut the rope, and tomorrow me and Beansie go to work in the mines."

Moaning in distress, Bill took a deerskin purse from his pocket and fished out two ten-dollar gold pieces. "And there's at least twenty dollars' worth of groceries in them boxes, too," he said. "You two will break me. You're after my heart's blood, Honker."

They lowered the beef carcass into the wagon and watched Bill drive off with it. Honker handed Beansie one of the gold pieces.

"All mine!" Beansie sighed. "I cain't believe it!"

"That's what I mean by plunder," said Honker. "We plundered him afore he could plunder us. But it's still just wages, and don't you ever forget that. Nobody ever got rich working for wages. Can you cook?"

"Sure, I'm a good cook, sir."

"Where'd you learn?"

"I don't think that makes no difference, does it?"

"Depends on how good a cook you are. Go on, get us some supper. Because I sure don't intend to."

They ate fresh liver fried with onions, baking-powder

biscuits, gravy, and canned plums for supper. With a freshly whittled toothpick in his mouth, Honker leaned back in his chair and put his elbow on the table. "Now, let's talk about where you learned to cook, boy," he said.

"I ain't going to tell you."

"From your mama, I'll bet."

"I said I ain't going to tell you."

"You don't have to. Them was noble biscuits, Beansie, but I've knowed dozens of cow-camp cooks that could do as good. Frying liver, though, takes a touch like playing the organ. Not many men can do it. Then you take the gravy: you gave yourself away there too. Your mama taught you how to make gravy, didn't she?"

Beansie leaned on the table and forced himself to meet those malevolent amber eyes. "You look here now, Mr. Cahoon. I don't pester you about your private affairs, and I ain't going to have you pestering me. If you don't leave me alone, I'll leave you and get a job somewhere."

"Boy, you might as well tell me. I'll get it out of you sooner or later."

"You just want to make me go back home. I bet you think my family's got a reward out for me!"

Honker pointed the toothpick at him. "Beansie, if I could make five hundred dollars just by riding down to Sacramento to wire your family where you are, I wouldn't waste sweating my horse on it."

"Then why do you keep pestering me, sir?"

"I like to know who I'm pardnered up with. For all I know, you're a wholesale murderer. But we can drop that whole proposition now. Little by little, I'm finding out all I need to know about you. I reckon we're going to get along all right. One man in every pardnership ought to be able to cook, and I sure can't."

"Do I have to do the dishes too?"

"Sure."

"I don't see why."

"You're plunder, kid. I furnished the Indians to do our work for us, didn't I?"

"I don't think that's very fair."

"I don't think so either, but this is how a man gets rich. Now, go wash your dishes, boy, and leave me be. I declare, you're the worst boy to argue."

Beansie woke up several times during the night, to see Honker still sitting in his chair beside the table, his dark, Satanic face engraved with a scowl. When Beansie woke up at daylight, Honker was asleep in the chair. He looked so pitifully old and tired and defenseless, the boy hated to disturb him. He dressed quietly and went outside.

The fog was so thick it was hard to see the heavy corral posts a hundred feet away. Beansie cared for the horses and brought in an armload of wood. He had breakfast ready when a groan behind him told him that Honker was awake.

Honker stumbled sleepily to the door, opened it, and looked out. The thick fog carried sound incredibly. The rumble of the stamping mill, at the mine three miles away, sounded right next door.

"Hear that, Beansie?" said Honker.

"Yes. It don't bother me none."

"It does me. That machine is pounding out money for somebody but not for the men that work there. Not for you. Not for me."

"Breakfast is ready."

"Yes, you and me are just working stiffs. Ten dollars a day is better than two or three, but not much."

"Set down and eat. There's pancakes and gravy and

more liver, and fresh coffee. You'll feel better when you've et, Mr. Cahoon."

"I don't want to feel better! The discontented man is the one that gets rich. We've got to go over and bring back some more cattle this morning, like a couple of old cheap cowboys. Wash the dishes, and let's go."

The fog became a drizzle as they crossed the narrow valley. Beansie shivered in his worn clothing and tried not to let Honker see how uncomfortable he was. Not that Honker showed any interest in anything. He rode with his chin on his chest, his mouth locked in an angry sneer. Boy, I'd sure hate to be some trouble making gunman that tried to start anything with him now, Beansie thought with a swell of pride. He must be the meanest man in the world. . . .

The sun broke out as they climbed the western pass. Blue jays surrounded them, scolding loudly. A fat old she-bear, already thinking about where to den up for the winter, waddled across the trail ahead of them. They were never out of sight of fat deer.

They reached the summit in an hour's hard riding and started down into the prettiest little valley that Beansie had ever seen. It was dotted with fenced haystacks, crisscrossed with fences. The fat Zigzag T cattle did not number in the thousands, but they were in prime condition. And above all, they were close to the Pacific ports and the markets of the world.

"What does Mr. Shenker want with any more money?" said Beansie. "When I get rich this is exactly the kind of place I'm going to buy."

"There ain't no place like this," Honker said. "If there was, it wouldn't make you happy."

"Yes it would."

"No, the more you have, the more you want. The man who only owns what he can wear at one time and ride at one time and eat in a day—he's happiest."

"Then why do you want to get rich?"

"Because all my life I never knowed how happy I was. Now I want to try it the other way and be rich and miserable."

"That don't make sense to me, sir, if you'll excuse me."

Honker did not answer. Another hour's riding brought them to the Zigzag T's home place. It was deserted by all but the aged and infirm, every able-bodied man having quit to prospect for gold or silver or work in the hard-rock mine at Camp Corinth. An old man with a wooden leg came out to meet them.

He and Honker remembered each other from ten years ago. "There's better than a hundred in the corral eating their heads off, Honker," the man said. "All I do is fork hay to them. I didn't know you was a butchering hand."

"A man can do anything he has to," Honker said evasively.

"Yes. Like Smoky O'Neill—remember when he got a chance to work for the telegraph? Learned the telegraph code in one night, by gum. He had this big family eating him out of house and home."

"I wonder what Smoky's doing now."

"Still working for the telegraph. I seen him last month when I was in Sacramento for Bill. He's just making ends meet, but a man with a family like his'n, he can't take a chance and leave a steady job."

They took the first fifteen out of the gate and started

them on the eastward trail. "That shows you," Honker said, "what chance a poor man has."

"What does?"

"Smoky O'Neill. He knows everything about the electric. He can make you a battery out of a glass fruit jar and things from the drugstore if he has to."

"I heard of that, sir. I never seen anything that was electric though."

"I have, and I don't like it. It never did scare Smoky O'Neill though. I reckon Smoky's so smart he has to sleep with his feet higher than his head so his brain can soak up extra blood. He has forgot more than you and me ever will know."

"I don't want anything to do with the electric," said Beansie. "I knowed a man that catched hold of one of them wires once, and he said it like to jerked him loose from his teeth before he could let go."

"Well, the electric sure didn't make Smoky O'Neill rich. It ain't brains you need to make money. There's lots of rich men as ignorant as us. Look at Bill Shenker. I never met anybody as dumb as him, and yet he's stacking up five thousand dollars a day. *Five thousand dollars a day*, Beansie."

"About a dollar a day from every man in Camp Corinth," Beansie said thoughtfully. "I reckon you've got to take some kind of a grip on fate and hang on and not let anything but getting rich be on your mind."

Honker did not answer. He did not, in fact, speak another word until they were across the ridge and the cattle were in the corral by Fat Tree Creek. The Washos had heard them coming. One hour after the gate was closed, three beef carcasses were swinging from the tackle in the trees. It was not much past noon.

"I'll go fix us something to eat," Beansie said.

Honker nodded absently. He unsaddled the horses and forked some hay to them. The Washos straggled off into the timber. Honker drove his pitchfork into the ground and leaned on it, his mind toiling painfully over the hopeless prospect of ever pulling in enough to keep him comfortable in his old age, let alone make him rich. He tried in vain to recapture the elated excitement of yesterday.

No use. Honker thought, I'm one of the meek ones, always a-slipping and a-sliding around to keep anybody from noticing me, dreaming the daydreams of a born coward. And then, just so's somebody will think well of me, bragging and boasting fit to get me killed dead someday! I ain't nobody, and I never had nothing, and I never will—

A piercing, echoing shriek from the cabin made his raw nerves tingle. He sprinted for the door, snatching out his .45 as he ran. The bloodcurdling noise went on and on and on. He flung open the cabin door.

Apparently Beansie had gone mad. He was racing around the cabin, tearing off his shirt without bothering with the buttons. He had already kicked off his boots. Now the shirt came off too. He hurled it to the floor and sank down on one of the cowhide chairs, holding up his pants, which had been about to fall.

"What in thunder!" said Honker.

Beansie stared at him with haunted eyes and panted hoarsely, "Mice! Millions of mice! One of the dad-blamed varmints ran right up the leg of my pants and got into my shirt."

"You mean that's what all that bellering was about?"

Beansie retrieved his shirt sheepishly. "I don't mind a

mouse now and then—no sir! But I don't like whole herds of them, and I don't want them inside of my clothes with me. Mr. Cahoon, this place is just full of mice! Look at the holes in this floor! And they've already et through the grocery sacks. They're into everything!"

"Beansie, mice always chaw their way into a cabin, and the minute you light a fire after the cold weather starts, they move in on you from miles around. What do you expect, boy?"

"They'll eat more of our grub than we will."

"What do you care? Bill Shenker pays for it."

Beansie snatched up a chunk of firewood and hurled it across the cabin. The mouse he was aiming at slid into the nearest hole in the plank floor.

"*A-a-a-ah!*"

The wordless, choking gasp came from Honker. Now it was Beansie's turn to stare in alarm as Honker tottered to the other chair and sat down in it. Beansie jumped up and clutched Honker by the arm.

"Mr. Cahoon, are you all right?"

Honker waved him off, but it took him a second or two to catch his breath. "I'm all right. Let me alone while I think."

"I thought you was having a heart attack."

Honker leaped to his feet, thrust his hands into his pockets, and began clumping back and forth the length of the cabin. "More like a brain attack. I just remembered something from ten years ago. Oh Lordie, I only hope it ain't too late."

"Too late for what, sir?"

Honker did not answer but continued pacing with his hands in his pockets. Beansie returned to his cooking, keeping a wary eye out around his boots.

"I'll put some beans on to boil for supper," said Beansie, "but the mice has been in the bacon, and I'll have to trim most of it away unless you don't mind taking seconds after the mice."

No answer.

"All I can fix for now is eggs and fried potatoes, and the mice has been in the potatoes too."

No answer.

"Lucky they ain't learned how to suck eggs yet, but they will. I expect to crack an egg any day and find a mouse curled up inside, having a nap after his meal."

Honker seemed to come out of a deep trance. "Fix me something to eat, boy—anything that's fast. I've got to go into Camp Corinth," he said.

"Mr. Cahoon," Beansie said indignantly, "you didn't hear a word I said."

"I did too."

"All right then, what did I say?"

"You said the cabin was full of mice."

Beansie saw that Honker really had not taken in a word he had said about the food. He reached for the skillet with one hand, the eggs with another.

"I wonder," Honker said, "if there's any writing paper around here."

"No," said Beansie. "Why should there be?"

"I'll get some in Camp Corinth somewhere."

"Get some mousetraps too."

"You forget about trapping them poor little mousies! Shame on you, boy! Do you begrudge the meekest and shyest little varmint in the animal kingdom a few bites of grub?"

"They ain't meek and shy, and I told you, they're eating more of our grub than we are!"

"Beansie, I heard about a fella once that was kind to a poor little mouse and fed it and gave it a warm place to sleep, and so forth. Well then, some time later, this fella had some bad luck and got tied up by bandits—"

"I know, and the mouse came along and chewed his ropes in two. I never did believe that story nohow."

"All the same, leave our mice alone! There's nothing cheerfuller on a cold night than a gang of mice squeaking and fighting and scratching the floor under the bed. Don't argue with me, boy. Leave them mice alone!"

He really meant it. Maybe the old coot was going loco. . . .

CHAPTER FIVE

They could hear the firing before Camp Corinth came into sight. It sounded like several six-guns, and at least four or five shots from each. There were a couple of howls of anger—and then, after the shooting stopped, the ominous, rising growl of an angry mob.

Honker instinctively reined in. All his life it had been his nature to depart, instantly and rapidly, in the other direction, when such unseemly sounds arose. Whenever there was violence of any kind, Wilber W. Cahoon was never found among those attending. But Beansie dug in his heels and shouted back over his shoulder as his horse broke into a dead run.

"Hey, did you hear that? A gun fight, a gun fight! I never seen a real gun fight. Come on!"

The shooting and shouting died as suddenly as it had started. Honker let his horse trot after Beansie's. It was still not the kind of mess he liked to witness, but the crisis appeared to be over, and a man had to take a certain amount of risk if he meant to become rich.

The mob was straggling back down the street on foot, grumbling in frustration. Bill Shenker was unloading his bull wagon in front of the Silverado. He gave them a surly, suspicious look and swung a hundred pounds of sugar up on his shoulder.

Honker pulled in his horse and hooked a leg around

his saddle horn. "Howdy, Bill," he said. "Breaks my heart to see a man as rich as you dirtying his hands with honest labor. Your face is so red, you could drop dead."

Bill heaved the sack of sugar to a man inside the Silverado. "You's supposed to drive some steers over from the home place today," he said.

"We did."

"Then you's supposed to butcher three of them."

"We did."

Bill gaped at them. "I don't believe you! That's a dad-blamed lie!"

"You call a man a liar, you ort to be ready to back it up. You want me to bet you a hundred dollars on it? You can go get your meat any time."

Bill shouldered another hundredweight of sugar and carried it to the door of the Silverado. "Just no sense in a man in my position having to do this," he panted, "but if you want a job done, you have to do it yourself."

"Not when you depend on me and Beansie. We're prob'ly the only men in these mountains you can trust, Bill."

"And I don't trust you very far, Honker. But it's sure the truth: something happens to a man's soul in a mining camp. All anybody thinks of is money, money, money."

"I reckon you're the only human person left in camp that's free from the sinful scourge of greed. What was all the gunplay about?"

"Oh, just a couple of horse thieves."

"I take it they got plumb away."

"Sure. I try to tell these other businessmen we got to hire us a lawman, but they won't do it."

"And I bet I know what they tell you. They say you're

making most of the money in camp—you ort to pay most of his wages."

"Well, dag-nab it, Honker, fair is fair! We all ort to chip in, dollar for dollar. I don't ask them how much they make; what business is it of theirs what I make?"

"Bill, there's two ways of figuring everything—the rich man's way and the poor man's. One of these days some disrespectful highwayman that don't know his place is going to rob you of half a day's ill-gotten gains and you'll wish you had figgered it the other way."

A worried look flitted across Bill's face, but then he clamped his jaw shut again. "No sir! I ain't paying nobody else's share of nothing," he said between his teeth.

Honker got down off his horse. "Let's tie here in front of Bill's place, where no horse thief is going to take liberties with a man's property, and take a look at this gilded den of iniquity of Bill's. I want you to see just how grand this man's soul is, Beansie."

The Silverado's striped tent was literally bulging at the seams, but Honker put his head down and forced his way through the crowd, with Beansie following in his wake. To the left was the long bar, tended now by four bartenders. Over their heads hung the uncompromising notice *All Drinks $1*, but there was no lack of trade.

To the right of the entrance was the restaurant. Honker ignored it as well as the bar. After catching his breath, he drove through the crowd to the back of the tent, which held three poker tables and one dice table. Honker went straight to the dice table.

"Know anything about craps, Beansie?" he whispered.

"I ain't interested in gambling. You can't get rich if you gamble."

"That ain't necessarily true. If you're the house man, rich is the only thing you can get—at least here."

"Why, are the dice crooked?"

"Not these, I reckon. Oh—if somebody stands to win a lot of money on one throw, they'd prob'ly switch in the weights on you. But look at the odds."

He pointed to the sign above the stick man's head. "Don't mean a thing to me," Beansie said.

"For instance, he pays only three to one on a hardway ten—two fives. It should pay ten to one. And look—a dollar limit on bets, and you can only pyramid five times. Then you have to start over at the dollar limit."

"That don't mean nothing to me, either."

Honker said patiently, "Pyramiding is letting your money lay and betting your winnings when you've got a lucky streak going. If you start with a dollar and pyramid five times, you end up with thirty-two dollars, and a dollar of that is your own money, see?"

"That's a lot of profit on one dollar, Mr. Cahoon."

"For five straight passes? What it means is, If you get a lucky streak going, they cut you off just when it starts to pay off. If you could hit five more passes in a row and pyramided your bets, you'd have a thousand and twenty-four dollars, including your own dollar."

"Gee whiz!"

"But Bill cuts you off at thirty-two dollars and makes you start over. He'll bleed you to death with them small bets, but you never get a shot at his bankroll. This is the worst deadfall craps game I ever seen."

"Then why are they so anxious to play it? Look at them, fighting to get up there to bet their money."

"Son," Honker said sorrowfully, "when you're a miner, you go around begging somebody to take your money.

I don't know why Bill bothers with these games. He ort to just put a basket out in front with a sign on it: '*Drop Money Here. No Torn Bills Accepted!*' Let's try our hand at this sport of his."

Honker put a gold piece down and received ten chips. He lost them all without ever getting his hands on the dice. He left the craps table without comment, and Beansie followed him to one of the poker tables. Above them hung another sign:

No Money Lending—House Banks Everybody!
Chips Only—Cash Pots Prohibited.
No Wild Card Games—Straight Draw & Stud Only!
New Deck Costs $5 in Advance.
Keep the Game Moving. Others May Want to Play!

Beansie did not need to be told that the house man was the player with the box of chips and the big stacks of money in front of him. There were six chairs at a table, with a waiting line behind each.

The ragged hard-rock miner behind whom Honker stood chunked his last chip into the game. "I'll borry ten," he said.

"Twenty-five is the smallest loan we make, my friend," said the house man. "Sign here."

He pushed a marker across the table. The miner signed it, but Beansie noticed that the house man counted out only twenty chips. Either the miner did not notice, or he did not care.

He lost the money quickly. Honker and Beansie moved on. "Hey, Mr. Cahoon—did you notice that he cheated that fella out of five dollars?" Beansie whispered.

"No, he didn't," said Honker. "The other five is interest on the loan, paid in advance. Yes sir, Bill Shenker is one cautious gambler. If he's taking in less than ten thousand a day in this camp altogether, I'm the granddaughter of a one-eyed Potawatomi medicine man. Let's go look the great man up. Something I want to talk with him about."

They found Bill out by his bull wagon again. He was taking a long black cigar from his coat pocket. Honker approached and said, "Howdy again, Big-hearted Bill!"

"Howdy, Honker," Bill replied absently.

Honker put out his hand. Without thinking, Bill put the cigar into it. Honker put it in his mouth and leaned forward for a light. Bill, his mind still on something else, struck a match and lighted it for him.

He did not notice what had happened until Honker puffed out a big cloud of smoke. "Hey, what are you doing with my cigar?" he shouted then.

"Not bad for a cheap smoke," said Honker. "I was wondering, Bill, where your roulette wheel is."

"You can't run a wheel without keeping an eye on it, and I got too much else to do. Your crew will steal you blind. I got enough trouble as it is."

"But a gambling hall ain't a gambling hall, without a wheel. Roulette is the only game played all over the world, didn't you know that?"

"I know it," Bill said with a grimace of pain, "and there's some people won't bet on anything but roulette, but what can I do?"

"I still think you ort to put in roulette."

"No! I wouldn't fool with it nohow."

Honker put his hand on Beansie's shoulder. "You heard that, boy," he said, his eyes glittering strangely. "You're a witness that he said he wouldn't have roulette nohow."

"What do you mean by that?" Bill demanded.

"Nothing. Thanks for the cigar, Bill. Say!"

"What now?"

"Say, what would you do if somebody put in a roulette wheel here?"

"I'd only wish him luck. If you could make money off'n a roulette wheel, I'd have one myself."

Bill turned his back on them. Honker set off down the muddy street with Beansie. "You heard that now. You heard him say he'd only wish them luck," Honker muttered.

"Mr. Cahoon, what are you up to?" Beansie asked.

"A crumb from the rich man's table mebbe."

"You mean Bill Shenker?"

"I don't know no other rich men here, do you?"

"I was just thinking, Mr. Cahoon. Bill seems so miserable, maybe it's the wrong idee, to get as rich as him. Maybe medium rich is about right for us."

"It don't work out that way, son. That's a trip you go all the way, or you don't even get a good start. Unless your soul is full of greed, ain't no use even trying."

"Is your soul full of greed?"

"I don't honestly know, Beansie. I got a strange feeling that it's filling up. Here's the Wells Fargo. Let's go in here."

The Wells Fargo tent, although by no means the largest on the street, was one of the sturdiest. The man behind the counter was armed by two .45s hung in crisscrossed cartridge belts. A .30-30 rifle and a 12-gauge shotgun hung in a rack behind him.

"When's your next trip to Sacramento?" Honker asked him.

"Early tomorrow. One goes every day."

"And I reckon one comes back every day too?"

"Well, I'd play the dickens sending an outfit out of here if one hadn't come in the day before, wouldn't I?"

"Can I send a draft for a hundred dollars out to somebody in Sacramento?"

"If you got the hundred dollars. It's a two-day trip. He'll have it day after tomorrow."

Honker squatted down and began fishing gold pieces out of the slits in the double tops of his boots. He ordered a draft for one hundred dollars to Smoky O'Neill and then paid a dollar for paper, an envelope, and the use of a pencil.

He spent so long writing his letter that Beansie grew restless and left the tent. He had not gone more than a hundred yards down the street when he heard a gunshot. There was just the one, and then—silence for a moment.

A man began groaning, and a crowd boiled out of a tent not far down the street from Beansie. Two of the men were supporting a third, whose left leg dripped blood copiously.

"Right in here—right next door. There's a new doctor here," someone shouted.

They went into a tent over which hung a sign identifying the occupant as Dr. J. Sumner Wheelwright. Beansie tried to push in behind them, but the crowd was too great. He could hear the patient groan now and then, but there was too much noise for him to make out what was happening.

"Don't fret, young man. I only nicked him in the meat. He'll have a little dimple to remember me by, but that's all," a voice said behind Beansie.

He turned and saw a well-dressed man with a face like something whittled out of hardwood, and eyes like two

chips of ice. He wore a handsome frock coat, open to
show the gun belt across his flat lower belly. The gun itself was not visible, but Beansie could see the bottom of
the holster. It was tied, gunman-fashion, to the man's leg.

"Criminy! Are you a quick-draw artist?" Beansie
breathed.

The stranger smiled without mirth or warmth. "I have
been called that here and there."

"What happened, he try to draw on you?"

"Him? Certainly not! Those three merely tried to pick
my pocket. Oldest game in the world, son. One stops in
front of you to block your way, the other blunders into
you—hard—and knocks you into the first one, and the
third one lifts your poke while you're off balance. They
won't try it again for a while."

"Crikers, I bet not! There's another famous gunman
in town, did you know that?"

A shadow whipped across the stranger's hard face and
was gone. "No, I did not. Happen to know his name?"

"Honker Cahoon."

"Don't believe I have ever heard of him."

"I can take you to meet him!"

The stranger shook his head. "That's kind of you, but
I'll pass up that pleasure. I have never heard of your
champion and have no interest in shaking his hand. If
he has heard of me and cares to make a personal call, all
he has to do is look for me. I'm never hard to find."

"Yes," said Beansie, "but would you mind telling me
your name, so I can tell him?"

The man merely smiled and sauntered on. Beansie
watched him go, torn between admiration and regret,
thinking, Gee whiz, he can't be much if he never even
heard of Honker Cahoon. But I bet you anything, he's a

killer. I never met one before, but them eyes of his—oh my, a new-born baby would know by his eyes . . .

"You sure have got your gall," a man said to him.

"Me? Why?" said Beansie.

"Asking him for his name. That's just about the worst insult you can hand a gunman like him. You're supposed to *know* a gunnie's name."

"I didn't though. Do you?"

"Sure. That's Dewey Score."

That's impossible because he don't know Mr. Cahoon, was Beansie's first thought. His second was, No, maybe he was just pretending. He wouldn't want to admit that Honker Cahoon made him back down. I better go tell Mr. Cahoon that Dewey Score's in town. . . .

But Honker was nowhere to be found. Neither was his horse.

Honker had finished transacting his business with Wells Fargo and had come out to look for Beansie, when he overheard, from somebody's excited conversation, the magic words: "Dewey Score's in town. He just shot a pickpocket!"

Honker remembered hearing a shot while he was finishing his letter, but he had been too interested in the job of sealing it, and in the draft inside the envelope, to know or care what was going on outside the tent.

The moment he heard the name Dewey Score, his mind flitted back to the tale he had told Beansie. He had never laid eyes on the famous gunman and had no idea what he looked like. Nor did he, at this moment, really care.

But sauntering down the street toward him, not more than a hundred feet away, came a hard-faced stranger about his own age and size, well-dressed in a frock coat that hung open over two crossed belts. No fairy had to whisper in Honker's ear to identify the apparition for him.

One step took him back inside the Wells Fargo tent. As the well-dressed gunman was passing the tent, Honker was slipping out under it at the rear, unseen even by the Wells Fargo agent.

Two minutes later he was whipping his horse out of Camp Corinth, heading not for Bill Shenker's beef camp but back on the trail toward the Mokelumne and then Nevada. He forgot all about his ten-dollar-a-day job, his plans for getting rich, and the letter and draft he had just sent to Smoky O'Neill in Sacramento. He forgot even Beansie.

It was the memory of Beansie that made him haul his horse down and sit for what seemed like hours in a torment of indecision. Had anyone challenged him, he could not have said what he thought he could do for Beansie that the boy could not do for himself, but he still felt some sort of odd, nagging responsibility for him.

Thus when Beansie had given up searching and got back to the cabin a couple of hours later, he found Honker cheerfully splitting firewood for the stove.

"Hey, you better let me do that, sir," Beansie said. "You can stiffen up your hands on an ax, and you shouldn't do that with Dewey Score in town."

Honker split another chunk of fat pine and then stopped to lean on the ax. "Oh, Dewey's in town?"

"Yes sir, and I talked to him. Honest I did—me, my own self! I was so close I could've touched him. But you know what he said, Mr. Cahoon? He said he had plumb never heard of you!"

"Oh, he did, did he? He said that, did he?"

"Yes."

"I tell you what, Beansie: let's just leave it at that, shall we? He's prob'ly happier than if he had good sense."

The boy smiled so widely that his eyes snapped. "He's just pretending, ain't he? He thinks he can nerve himself up for another showdown with you, don't he?"

"I 'spect that's right."

"Jeeminy! He sure is going to get the surprise of his life, ain't he? I'll go get us some supper, Mr. Cahoon. You know what? I thought he looked just plain, pure poison, he was so mean. But you're really just sort of amused, ain't you?"

"I reckon you could say that, Beansie."

The boy took care of his horse and went into the cabin, where again Honker heard him reviling the mice at the top of his voice. Honker was all right until he tried to drive the ax into a tree, to put it away for the night. When he took the first step, his knees started to cave in on him. He had to clutch wildly at the tree to keep from falling.

Why do I do it? Why—why—why—?

CHAPTER SIX

What appeared to be a mass meeting of some kind was going on when Beansie rode into Camp Corinth late the following morning. They were using Bill Shenker's bull wagon for a speakers' platform, and at least five or six hundred men were jammed around it. The speaker was a man Beansie had never seen before, but obviously he wasn't a miner. The boy reined in to listen.

"If them that should take the responsibility won't take it, they got to be forced. They's only one way to do that. It's a mighty desperate plan, but I'm tired of being robbed and beat up, and I'm ready to go the limit. We're all at the mercy of outlaws until we get some law and order here," the speaker shouted.

He had the crowd with him, to judge by the yells that arose from it:

"Yay, law and order—that's what we need!"

"Go to it, Sandy. We'll back you all the way."

"What's your plan, Sandy? I'm for it!"

"Law and order, law and order!"

"Give 'em hell, Sandy! You got the right idee."

Sandy paused to catch his breath and mop his forehead. He held up his hand for silence and got it. He began speaking again:

"Won't do us any good to elect some leading citizen our city marshal. We tried that before, and it just don't work in this town. No, what we need is the meanest, toughest man we can get for the job. I say pay him five hundred a month and let *him* collect it from the merchants and businessmen. I'll be glad to pay my share, and I'll tell you this: If he ain't tough enough to collect his own pay, he ain't tough enough to keep the peace here."

"Go to it, Sandy! I second the motion."

"Now you're talking sense, Sandy."

Another man got the crowd's attention. "I like the idee, yes I do, but what I want to know is this: How are we going to know if the man we elect is tough enough to keep the job? Suppose somebody tougher comes along?"

"Then we'll have us a new city marshal, that's what," Sandy replied. "Same way, if *two* men apply for the job instead of one. We'ns don't have to choose between them. Let *them* settle it!"

"The more I hear of your idee," the other man shouted, "the more I see that you have thought it through to the bitter end. Five hundred a month is a lot of money, gents, but I've been robbed of more than twice that much so far, and no end in sight. I move we vote on it now. All in favor of Sandy's plan, to hire the toughest man we can find, and pay him five hundred dollars a month and let him collect it—say 'aye.'"

The roar of ayes made it unnecessary to call for the dissenting vote. There was a little commotion around the wagon, and then Bill Shenker came climbing up the front wheel. He held up his hands for attention.

(Crikers, Beansie was thinking—I ort to hurry back and tell Mr. Cahoon. Five hundred a month is a lot more than he's making now, and we could prob'ly keep this job too. And there sure couldn't nobody beat him if it came to a showdown over being marshal. . . .)

Bill Shenker was saying, "You tarnation idiots, do you realize what you just done? You put us all at the mercy of any bullying gunman who comes to Camp Corinth. I tell you one thing sure: I ain't going to pay no part of a subscription to pay his wages."

It appeared to Beansie that violence might break out, Bill Shenker and a few of his hired hands against everybody else in Camp Corinth. It seemed to him that they needed Mr. Cahoon even more than they realized. He had turned his horse, to trot back out to the cabin, when a new voice joined the debate.

"Gentlemen, gentlemen! Your kind attention, if you please. I believe I can short-cut your disagreements and solve your problem for you."

"Who asked you?" Bill Shenker shouted back. "You keep out of this. You ain't no businessman in this camp!"

The crowd parted to let the peacemaker through. He clambered up the wheel of the bull wagon and dropped down between Bill and Sandy. Beansie muttered, "Whoo-eee!" to himself, and decided to wait to hear the rest of it.

The new debater was the well-dressed man in the frock coat—the old gunman who had once been Beansie's hero, Dewey Score. A few men in the crowd might have recognized him, because Beansie heard some uneasy grumbling, but most did not.

"What's your proposition, stranger? And make it quick, because we got official business to transact," said the merchant Sandy.

"My proposition is to take the job myself, keep the peace, and collect my own pay of five hundred dollars a month. And to demonstrate that I'm the man for the job, I'll start now by collecting from Bill Shenker."

"The hell you will!" Bill whooped.

"Don't make me prove it! Your assessment will be—well, let's see—about five times the amount of every other merchant in Camp Corinth. They'll pay me five dollars a month, and you'll pay twenty-five, starting today."

"Who the hell do you think you are?" Bill said, when he could say anything.

"I don't think—I *know*. The name is Dewey Score. Gold, please, Mr. Shenker—no currency, checks, drafts, letters of credit, or due bills. *And I'll have it now*, if you please!"

In a way it was a beautiful thing to see. Beansie thought at first that Bill Shenker might stand there in plain view of everybody and choke to death on his own tongue. But he finally got his poke out, fished out the gold pieces, and handed them over. Score thanked him with a curt nod and turned to face the crowd again.

"This meeting is adjourned. There will be no more mass meetings, is that clear? Go to your places of business. I will shortly call on each of you to collect the five dollars for this month's assessment. All right now, gents—clear the street, clear the street!"

The crowd melted away like a snowbank under a sudden sun. Of those in the crowd who did not recognize Dewey Score, a few obviously had never heard of him either, but they got the word—in urgent whispers, quickly. The man himself, standing in the bull wagon, alone now, was as impressive as his reputation. His beady eyes flitted over the crowd, and wherever those eyes paused, there was a quick commotion.

Beansie again turned his horse, to hurry out to the cabin and tell Honker. At the last moment, he remembered that he had not taken care of the chore that had brought him into Camp Corinth in the first place.

Mr. Cahoon had acted very strange this morning. He

was anxious to make sure his letter had gone down to Sacramento, but he could not go into town himself. He had things on his mind, he said vaguely. Plans to make, if they ever intended to get rich here.

Beansie tied his horse in front of the Wells Fargo tent and went inside. Yes, the agent said, the letter had left early that morning and would be in Sacramento tomorrow. Beansie turned to go.

Dewey Score came into the tent, and Beansie changed his mind. The new city marshal of Camp Corinth went up to the counter and tipped his hat politely.

"Your turn, sir," he said. "I find that all your fellow merchants are extremely co-operative, and if I may say so, this attitude will contribute to the pacification of Camp Corinth."

The Wells Fargo man may have turned a little pale. "Yes, Mr. Score," he said, "but I've got to stay out of this pot. My company don't make no provision for paying assessments like this."

"Indeed? I take it you weren't at the meeting in front of the Silverado a few minutes ago."

"I was there, but I—"

"You didn't object to the plan, did you? If so, I must have been suffering a moment of unconsciousness. I certainly don't remember hearing your objections."

"Wasn't no use objecting, Mr. Score, but that don't mean I have to go along with what they voted. My company furnishes its agents with all the necessary arms to protect ourselves, and if arms aren't enough, they send in extra men. And that, sir, is as fur as I can go."

"That's too bad. We mustn't be unreasonable."

"I'm mighty relieved you see it that way," the Wells Fargo man said. "You've got a kind of a quick-trigger reputation, Mr. Score, but it's plain to see you're a gentleman after all."

"I hope you are one, too," Score said, almost in a whisper, "because *you're* the one who mustn't be unreasonable. I'll have five dollars from you, sir, and I'll have it at once, without further argument."

"I'll see you in hell first!"

The agent reached for one of the weapons leaning against the counter on his side. Faster than the eye could follow, Dewey Score's hand went into his open frock coat. He leaned across the counter, the muzzle of a .45 in the agent's side before the man could get his hands on either his shotgun or carbine.

Score did not speak. He merely stood unmoving, his finger on the trigger and his thumb on the hammer of the gun. The only sound was the heavy breathing of the Wells Fargo agent.

"I'll have to reach into my pocket for my key," the agent said at last, in a trembling voice.

"Do so," said Score.

"I just wanted to make sure you wouldn't think I was reaching for no gun."

"I am quite sure you wouldn't do that, sir."

The agent got the key out of his pocket, unlocked the change till, and took out a five-dollar gold piece. He dropped it on the desk in front of them.

"I—I—" he choked.

"Yes?" Score said courteously.

"I wonder if I could ask you to sign a receipt for that. Maybe I'd have a chance of getting it back from the company. Otherwise it's out of my pocket."

"Delighted. Give me a piece of paper and a pencil."

Score read aloud as he wrote, "Received from Wells,

Fargo and Company the sum of five dollars, being the assessment for the current month for the engagement of the undersigned as City Marshal of Camp Corinth. Signed, Dewey Score, City Marshal."

"Thank you, sir."

"See you next month."

Score smiled at Beansie as he left the tent. The Wells Fargo man waited until he was long gone. Then:

"You seen that, boy, didn't you? We have turned a wolf into the sheep, that's what we have did. We have voted ourselves to be the victims of extortion at gun point. Let that be a lesson to you! Never trust the decision of a mob, because ninety-nine times out of a hundred it's going to be wrong," he said.

"Crikers!" said Beansie. "What's to stop him raising his own pay any time he feels like it? It's just as easy for him to collect a thousand dollars a month as it is five hundred."

"That's exactly what I mean. We stood there blatting like sheep at that meeting, and we deserve the wolf we introduced among us. What I'm ashamed of is that I knew it at the time—I knew it at the time—and said nothing."

This is sure a job for Mr. Cahoon, Beansie said to himself. None of this would've happened if he'd been here. I better let him know fast. . . .

He was up on his horse when he saw two riders trotting down the street toward him. They looked like plain old jobless cowboys, probably not the most peaceful citizens in the world but certainly not badmen. Then, just as the two rode past, Dewey Score came out of a tent after making another collection.

"Boys!"

He did not speak loudly, and he said only that one

word, but there was something penetrating about it that got to them instantly. Both men pulled in their horses and looked around. Sizing them up quickly, Beansie saw a tall man, gaunt and a little humpbacked but powerful-looking, and a shorter, chunkier, younger one.

"You speak to us, pardner?" the humpbacked man said.

"Yes. Let's shuck your guns now and stay healthy. We don't like a man to go armed here," Score said.

The tall man studied him. "I don't see no star on you, podner."

"That's right, you don't."

"Then how come you to give the orders?"

"I've been elected the marshal here. We're not going to talk about it no more, boys. Unbuckle your guns and hang them over your saddle horn. When you get where you're going, stow them in your duffle and don't take them out until you're out of town."

The two strangers exchanged quick glances. Again the humpbacked one did the talking.

"Reckon not, Marshal. We don't aim to make no trouble. Go up to the mine, see if they're hiring, and then decide what to do. Nobody bothers us, we won't bother nobody. Nothing wrong with that, is there?"

"Either take them off," Score said a little more loudly. He paused significantly before going on: "*Or draw them.*"

The humpbacked man said, "We're two to your one, but like I say, we ain't—*ha!*"

It happened so fast, Beansie had trouble trying to describe it to Honker that night:

"Mr. Score drawed both guns—*both* of them! He just kind of tipped his left-hand gun towards this younger fella, like to warn him not to cut himself in. He fired just once at the one with the humped back. Mr. Cahoon, I swear that tall fella knowed what was coming and retch for his gun first.

"It sounded like they fired at the same time, but Mr. Score like to shot this fella's shooting arm off. He shot it about halfway between the shoulder and the elbow. That gun flew halfway across the street, and the man almost fell off'n his horse.

"The other fella, he didn't make no move to mix in—not with Mr. Score holding his left-hand gun on him—not after seeing his pardner get winged that way. You just could hardly believe it, Mr. Cahoon, even if you seen it."

"Believe what?" Honker said. He lay on his back on his bunk, his boots off, his sock feet crossed. He stared at the ceiling without a change of expression.

"Believe that Mr. Score could pull both guns so fast and wing a man with one. That's a hard shot!"

"Yes it is, and you're right: I don't believe it."

"But I seen it!"

"Yes, but nobody can shoot that good, Beansie. I bet, if there was any way to find out the truth, he was shooting at this fella's guts and what he done was miss by a foot and a half."

"I don't think so. It was the dad-blamedest sight I ever seen in all my born days."

"Yes, and folks will be twice as scared of Dewey Score from now on, and he'll be twice as mean—and why? Just because he missed his shot by a foot and a half. What happened to these two poor cowboys?"

"They took the one to the doctor to get his arm sawed off, and the other one went with him."

Honker gave a snort that was half laughter. "I just won-

75

der how many men will dare to wear their guns on the street now. Nobody, I bet. He's got this whole camp begging him to line up and let them lick his hand now. I told you, Beansie, these gunmen are just trash. Just plain old riffraff that can't hold a job and haven't got a friend in the world. And now here is one of the richest mining camps in the world, right in the palm of Dewey Score's hand."

Beansie said uneasily, "Yes, and you know what, Mr. Cahoon? I just don't like that man at all. I bet you, everybody's going to be sorry they voted him in today, before they're through with him."

"Cinch."

"What you ort to do, Mr. Cahoon, is go into the camp there and throw the fear of the Lord into that Dewey Score before he goes too far. You're the only man in the natural world he's afraid of, sir. You don't have to have no shoot-out with him. I bet if you give him just one hard word, he'll be the tamest old gunman you ever seen. And yay, man—people sure would be grateful!"

Honker turned over on his side, rolling his eyes with an expression of intense agony. His eyes came into focus on Beansie's earnest face. His mouth worked as it tried to shape words he could not utter.

He came that close to confessing all—that close to saying, Beansie, I'm a coward and a liar, and I never seen Dewey Score before in my life, and I couldn't outdraw *you* with a six-gun! His soul was ripe for it, after all these tortured years, and it was not merely good for his soul; his common sense told him it would be healthier, too, in the long run.

He could not stay denned up out here at Bill Shenker's cabin the rest of his life, hiding from Dewey Score while

Beansie ran their errands in the camp. Sooner or later he had to go into town, and he had to do so without being under obligation to do the impossible—to face Dewey Score down and live up to what he had told Beansie about their imaginary past history.

The reason he did not confess all, but instead kept it bottled up inside him to his infinite discomfort and peril, was the look on Beansie's face. Such trust, such perfect faith, such downright adoration, were not for him to destroy. He flopped over on his back again, crossed his ankles, and stared up at the ceiling.

"I got other things to worry about than policing a dad-gummed disorderly mining camp," he said in his usual strident, honking tones.

"Something more important, you think, than maybe saving somebody's life?"

"Yes!"

"What could be more important than that?"

Again Honker rolled over on his side to face Beansie. "Do you want to get rich, kid, or don't you? I told you a dozen times, if you aim to get rich you can't let nothing stand in your way. You got to take aim like a mad bull, with only that one thing on your mind, and put your horns down and charge. I let you talk me into taking time out to punish this Dewey Score riffraff, we'll both ride out of here broke once the snow flies. Now don't bother me again about such things. I'm ciphering how to make us rich."

"I don't know as I want to be rich if that's the price of it," Beansie said. "What if I changed my mind about it—would you?"

"No."

77

"Not even to save somebody's life? I mean, I bet that Dewey Score is going to murder somebody if—"

"Beansie, it's too late," Honker said harshly. "We've got a partner to think of now too. Smoky O'Neill is tired of being broke, too, and he's got a family."

"Maybe this other fella has too."

"What other fella?"

"The one Dewey Score is going to murder unless you stop him."

"Yes sir, twelve little hungry kids, one of them just newborn, and one of them cross-eyed and needing an operation on his eyes, and the bank's about to foreclose on the water hole."

"How do you know all of them things?" Beansie cried wonderingly. "I don't even know who's going to get killed yet!"

"Neither do I, but it's just as easy to worry over a big family as it is a small one, when you have to make both of them up. Are your potatoes peeled yet?"

"No sir, but—"

"When you've got your work done, then you can set there and tell me how to do mine."

CHAPTER SEVEN

Bill Shenker had never been accused of being a sensitive, subtle man; in fact his reputation ran in exactly the opposite direction. For he was morose and solitary by nature, and his long sojourn in the mountains, where for most of the winter he saw only his own men, had emphasized his lone-wolf traits and his generally pessimistic outlook on life. He had always been content that things were no worse than they were during the years he was building up his Zigzag T herds. The idea of getting rich, really rich—offensively, disgustingly, and unimaginably rich—had never occurred to him.

He had been one of the first visitors to Fat Tree Creek after word of the hard-rock silver strike got out. He was not the adventurous type to hazard as much as fifteen minutes on a search for precious metal. All he had hoped for, on that first visit, was to sell a critter for beef.

One critter, one solitary sale, was as far as his ambition had flown. That was last fall, just before the high passes snowed in and closed off Fat Tree Creek and its valley to all but snowshoe traffic. He had found the boom in full swing, close to five hundred silver-crazed men camped along the creek. The syndicate had already bought the claims at Stairsteps, and had ordered heavy machinery for earliest spring delivery. By the time the snow closed the passes, Bill Shenker had moved his solitary bachelor household across the ridge to the cabin in the timber. He had brought along 150 grass-fat beef animals, in the modest hope of clearing perhaps as much as a thousand dollars on beef before spring.

It was impossible to prospect during the winter months, but the company could still drive tunnels. Every man stuck in the valley for the winter had gone to work in the hard-rock tunnels. They screamed like enraged Indians when Bill hiked the price of beef to eighty cents per pound, an unheard-of price even to the beef trust. The mining company had to raise their pay to compensate for the rise in the beef.

There was one encounter between Bill and the mine superintendent. The mining man represented money, power, and political influence; but since Bill negotiated from behind a double-barreled 12-gauge shotgun, the argument did not stretch out over any great period of time.

When spring thaws opened the passes again, the company's machinery was already coming up the western slope of the Sierra Nevada. So were two or three thousand men—nobody was sure how many. And Bill, who had been about to return to his ranch with a winter's profit of three thousand dollars—not a fortune, certainly, but three times what he had hoped to accumulate, was already there.

More important, Bill's avarice and ambition had been whetted by his one venture into high finance. He gave up any idea of returning to normal life at the Zigzag T, across the ridge, and determined to remain here and get rich. Unfortunately, lacking imagination, he had set his sights too low in the beginning. He had thought in terms of volume, not price.

He had not made as much money as Honker Cahoon

had estimated, but that was because of his late start in realizing how much the market would bear. His net profit was now running close to ten thousand dollars on a good day. But this was a recent development. He probably would never cease to mourn the missed opportunity, having seen, too late, the magical ten-thousand figure.

But he had done exceedingly well. He had a big steel safe in the Silverado, which he emptied several times a week. The contents went down by trusted night rider to a bank in Sacramento, where Bill's cash balance of $902,800 made him one of the richest men in America. It could just as easily have been $3 million—he knew that now.

He meant to store up an even million dollars before the snow flew again. His chances had been excellent—until Dewey Score's election as town marshal. In Marshal Score, Bill recognized a cupidity equal to his, and a mind that was probably a whole lot quicker to grasp opportunity. Score could not help but know, already, who was making all the money in Camp Corinth. If Bill was right about him, it would take him no more than a few hours to decide how to cut a slice of it for himself.

Bill was right. The evening of the day of Score's election, Bill was in his meat market, superintending the sale of the last of the day's beef. As usual the customers were grumbling. But they were buying beef, and paying in good gold coin.

A man sauntered in and stood just outside the circle of lamplight, puffing a fat black cigar. Bill broke into a cold sweat, and his hand trembled as he took in the gold and made change. When the last of the beef was gone, the town marshal was still there, puffing at his cigar. His face was not visible in the darkness, but Bill knew who it was.

He knew that Score wanted to get him alone, and he kept his meatcutter there as long as possible. It had to end sometime, and it did. The meatcutter took his fifty-dollar daily wages and departed, and Bill took the pad-locked cashbox under his arm. He went to the lamp that hung from the top of the tent and raised the globe to blow it out.

"Closing up for the night, stranger," he said, in a voice he wished were steadier.

"Not for a moment, sir. I want to have a moment or two of your valuable time."

"Oh, it's Mr. Score! You want to talk, walk on up to my other place with me, and—"

"Here is just fine," Score cut in softly. He put a hand out and tapped the cashbox with his fingertips. "I was watching your little graft in action, and I must say I admire you. Just how much is in that box?"

"I don't know. I didn't keep track."

"Well over three thousand, I'm sure. You really do run a big risk here, don't you? With so much money, and so many desperate drifters about, you're just asking to be stuck up. You know that, don't you?"

"Nobody has ever bothered me." Bill was beginning to sweat copiously, and the lamp was smoking. "I go armed, and I got a lot of friends in this camp that would hang a man that tried to stick me up. Come on, Mr. Score—let's get out of here and turn the ace over for today."

"You haven't got a friend in camp, Shenker," Score said. "I don't think anybody realizes just how much money you do keep around. These aren't thinking men, like you and me. All they're fit for is work and eat and booze it up. How many of them can even add enough figures to arrive at an idea of how much you take in each night? And yet if anybody took the time to add it up for them—"

"You've got no right to talk that-a-way. I don't bother with nobody else's business, and nobody bothers with mine. What do you want to suggest something like that for?"

"Because it's bound to happen, sooner or later. Bound to occur to someone that you're taking three to four thousand dollars in coin out of here every evening, and at least that much more out of the Silverado."

Bill's bowels turned to ice, but he had been made mad by ambition, and he was ready to risk death rather than give up on that magical million. He might have turned pale, but he shook his finger in Score's face, and his eyes narrowed and shone with a hard, starlike glitter.

"Don't you dare threaten me! I don't scare worth a damn. If you got anything to say, get it said, and get out of my store."

"I wouldn't try to scare you," Score murmured. "I was only thinking of your best interests. You're being too easy on these ignorant miners. As the only official in town, I think you ought to raise the price of beef another fifty cents."

"No. I tried it once. You can push people only so far. They'd lynch me."

"Maybe they would've then. They won't now. You now have a peace officer in town—remember?" Score patted the place where his two gun belts crossed. "I guarantee they'll pay two fifty a pound and make no trouble. Why, at another two bits a pound, you'll be taking in close to another thousand a day."

"I thought you said fifty cents a pound more?" Bill cried.

"I did. Twenty-five cents to you, twenty-five to me." Score stepped closer to Bill and jammed his forefinger into Bill's belly. His voice rose a little as he went on: "You ain't got nothing to think over, hear? Tomorrow the price goes up fifty cents, and I'll be around here at this same hour for my share."

"I tell you, they won't stand for it! The idee of making money is to know how fur you can push people. Why, there'll be a riot if I try it!"

"I told you, there will be no trouble."

Only he just don't know these people like I do, Bill thought. If it's a choice between them lynching me or him murdering me, I'll take my chances with him. . . .

"Nothing doing," he said flatly. "And if you think you can scare me with them two guns, guess again. I know how to take care of the likes of you."

"I suppose you mean Honker Cahoon," Score said.

"What?"

"I was told Cahoon was in town. He's supposed to be some punkins with a gun, I hear."

"He is?"

"Well, if that's how you're thinking, I reckon you and me will just have to put off our arrangement until me and Honker Cahoon have settled a few things. But don't you forget about it, Shenker, because I'll be back." Score squinted his eyes and flared his nostrils in silence for a moment. Then, *"I'll be back,"* he snarled, and walked out of the tent.

A bewildered and confused and frightened near-millionaire dazedly blew out the lamp, closed the flap of the tent, tucked the cashbox under his arm, and walked to the Silverado.

Honker Cahoon? he was thinking. Honker a gunman? That just don't seem reasonable to me, somehow. All I ever made him out to be was the loudest old bluffer that ever dodged a day's work—yes, and the biggest liar too. But maybe, just maybe, I misjudged him.

Certainly Dewey Score had demonstrated his respect for Honker, and from what Bill had heard, Score was pre-eminent in the art of killing a killer before he himself could be killed. Bill knew nothing about the terrible breed of the gunman except what he had heard in the gossip in his own bunkhouse. It was something men talked about in their idle moments, but these isolated mountains were not where notorious fast-draw artists spent their time. No, from what Bill had heard, they had to have an audience, people to fear and admire them, and to spread the word of each new high-speed feat of arms.

Was Honker a different kind of fast-draw artist and perhaps all the deadlier for it? It was something to think about, and not necessarily pleasantly. Bill remembered that he was already in Honker Cahoon's clutches, paying him and that kid a measly ten dollars a day apiece to keep him supplied with fresh-killed beef. Maybe it would be good sense to sort of suggest a little raise in pay tomorrow.

How could a man tell? The prospect of having to pay anything more out to anybody was heartbreaking. He was so near and yet so far from that magical million dollars. Yet by playing the tightwad with a few dollars, he might endanger the whole game.

One thing was sure, he dared not raise the price of beef to $2.50 per pound. On this subject Bill Shenker yielded to no man in expert knowledge. Men were strange, very strange. They had to have some kind of a quirk in them to risk their necks up here in the mining game in the first place. They were all go-for-broke gamblers, or they would not be here. They were all caught up in the frenzied dream of becoming rich, just as Bill was. They would put up with hard work, heat, cold, hunger, pain, every discomfort that could afflict the human body, in their fidelity to that dream. They gambled at crooked games and paid ungodly prices for the most ordinary things, because it was a sort of madness that distorted all values.

But they all had a point beyond which they would not be pushed, and Bill Shenker had risked a hanging once in this very matter. No other human being in the world was in the position of knowing, beyond the shadow of a doubt, that two dollars per pound was the limit human nature would stand for in the matter of beef, here on Fat Tree Creek, in Camp Corinth, California.

And if Dewey Score did not know that much, he was not as smart as he thought he was. The problem, from Bill's point of view, was to see to it that it was Score, not himself, who got caught with his pants down in any confrontation with the outraged citizenry of Camp Corinth. And that might take some doing.

As for Score, he had been far more shaken than he let Bill Shenker think when he walked out on their conference that evening. He had long ago lost his judgment of men, when he gave up his fraternity with them to become a fast-draw artist. He was not merely a loner; he was a different sort of creature. He was a predator who went about looking for prey, and for a challenge as much as a victim. And yet in his heart (or where his heart had

86

once been) there was always that secret, choking knowledge that someday, somewhere, he would meet a man just a shade faster and a shade luckier and his own long search would be over.

He had walked into Shenker's meat market with a light and buoyant step, with $715 in cash in his pocket, the biggest month's pay he had ever drawn in his life. He had had no trouble collecting it—$5 here, $10 there—after word got around about his showdown with the pickpockets. He was on top of the world!

When he looked back on that shooting this morning, he was not sure what had happened. He had drawn his gun wildly, an act of instinct, and did not remember pulling the trigger. Winging the miscreant was the luckiest thing that had ever happened to him, and he had been quick to bull the game to cash in on it.

He was so sure he could not lose when he went in to offer Shenker his proposition! He was the top man in camp—a wonderful thing to be—and this was his lucky day. What could go wrong? The perfect proposition. It would cost Shenker nothing—would, in fact, make him extra money—and having his protection would make Shenker eager to deal. It would be the fitting end to a grand day.

Instead Score had slunk out of the tent in a cold, quivering rage, close to the edge of a tantrum. He did not know what he most feared—murdering Bill Shenker in the fit and bringing this Honker Cahoon down on him with his gun blazing, or losing out on his glittering dream of wealth.

Score walked the length of the camp and then walked back, his spirit still uneasy and his problem unsolved. He pushed his way into the Silverado, rather hoping he

87

would not see Bill Shenker, because he did not know what his next move, if any, was going to be.

Bill was the first man he saw. He was behind the bar, serving out drinks and collecting the dollars as fast as his arms could make the motions. Their eyes met. Bill merely stared a moment, before letting his eyes drop. And Score thought, He has already talked to his man Cahoon. All right, I reckon tomorrow we'll find out who is the fastest, me or Cahoon. . . .

A cowboy by the name of Cory Chidester had just lifted his dollar drink and had turned sidewise to toss it down without getting it spilled by the crowd. Cory and Score had worked together for a rancher in New Mexico eight or ten years ago. That had been before Dewey Score earned his reputation as a gunman. He remembered Cory Chidester's face and name, and Cory remembered his.

They were not particularly glad to see each other. Score did not like to run into old acquaintances, who could remember when he was just another nothin' cowboy, and Cory did not like the reputation Score had acquired since they had last met.

"Hidy, Cory," Score said.

"Why, hidy, Dewey," said Cory. "Excuse me while I dump my load. Ain't hardly room enough to breathe here."

He drank his drink.

"Another one?" Score said. "On me."

"Don't mind if I do," Cory said, although what he really wanted was to get as far away from Score as he could.

Score flung a five-dollar gold piece on the bar and ordered doubles, and told the barkeep to keep the change.

"What brings you here, Cory?"

"Been working down in the Central Valley, and I wanted to get back east to Arizona before it snows. I ain't looking for no gold or silver, if that's what you mean."

"Neither am I. I'm the town marshal here."

"I be dogged! The town marshal, you say?"

"Yes. Cory, listen—you ever hear of a fella by the name of Honker Cahoon?"

"Why, I knowed him at one time, if it's the same one. Dark face with a scar on it, yella eyes, big black mustache, and a voice like a bull caught in the bobwire. That the one?"

"I ain't never met him myself. Is he some kind of a fast-draw artist with a gun?"

"I never seen him pull no gunplay myself, but he knows all the bad ones, and you hear about him all over the country. What I hear, he's just about the meanest and fastest there is, Dewey," said Cory.

"I see. Another drink?"

"No, I better not, thanks the same."

They parted, and Cory Chidester started down the trail toward the Mokelumne that very night. It would mean sleeping on the trail somewhere, but he wanted to be as far from Camp Corinth as possible, as soon as possible.

His memory of Honker Cahoon was dim, they having worked together only a few days on a place in Idaho, six or seven years ago. He had no recollection at all of Honker claiming to be a gunman, but that seemed to be on Dewey Score's mind, and Cory could not resist the temptation. He did not like gunmen, all of whom were bullies with, usually, other disagreeable traits. Dewey

89

Wayne Collis

seemed to be worried about Honker, and to give him something more to worry about had seemed like a good idea at the time.

Wonder whatever became of old Honker? the cowboy thought as his horse picked its way down the dark wagon road beside Fat Tree Creek. Kind of an old windbag, but no real meanness in him. And there sure is plenty in that Dewey Score. Only hope I didn't get old Honker into no trouble.

CHAPTER EIGHT

"You ride into Camp Corinth," Honker told Beansie early the next morning, "and see if that Wells Fargo man has heard anything from Sacramento. When you get back, we better go over the ridge for some more cattle."

Beansie had just put some beans on to boil with the bacon that Bill Shenker had supplied so reluctantly. It seemed to him that Mr. Cahoon was not being quite frank. In the first place it was too early to hear anything from Sacramento. In the second Honker did not look him straight in the eye as he usually did.

The kid knew better than to argue. He saddled up and gave his horse its head. It was another foggy morning in which sound carried clearly, but not a sound came from Camp Corinth, although the pounding of the mills over at Stairsteps was loud enough. When he reached the camp it was full of men, as usual.

But they were not making their usual racket. They minced along quietly, keeping a wary eye out on all sides. No sign of Dewey Score, but there was no question about his being responsible for the muted activity here. The whole town seemed to have decided that if Mr. Score was sleeping in today, it was better for all hands to let him sleep.

"Whoo-ee!" Beansie said softly to himself. "That fella sure has got this camp buffaloed. I reckon he's really a bad one."

Even Bill Shenker, preparing his bull wagon for an-other trip down the mountain for supplies, seemed to be walking on tiptoe. His driver, a grizzled, hard-faced old man who looked well able to take care of himself, leaned against the wagon wheel with his prod pole in his hand, declining to help hook up the two span of oxen. The shotgun guard that would ride with him was already up on the high seat of the wagon.

Ordinarily there was a commotion that drew huge crowds when Bill's wagon headed westward. Today Bill kept so silent that he practically whispered his orders.

His face lighted up when he saw Beansie, and after the bull wagon had started its long, slow trip down the muddy wagon road to the Mokelumne, he motioned for the kid to come over.

"Where's Honker today?" Bill wanted to know.

"Out to the cabin," Beansie replied. "It sure is quiet here, Mr. Shenker, ain't it?"

"So is the tomb," Bill replied gloomily. "There's such a thing as too much law and order, boy."

"I guess you mean Dewey Score."

"Yes. He has got this town under his thumb like I never thought a regiment of infantry could."

"Why don't you fire him as marshal?"

"Ha! There ain't a businessman here that wouldn't like that, but who's going to do it? One day, and they're all like kicked dogs."

The man called the Perfessor—Judson Blythe—came out of the Silverado, wiping his mouth with the back of his hand. Bill gave him a sour smile.

"Only one drink this morning, Perfessor?" he asked.

"One only," Blythe replied.

"That won't hardly start your blood to pumping, will it?"

"No," Blythe said with his engaging grin, "and it won't make me reckless enough to take chances with our new town marshal. When I'm feeling good, I have been known to give utterance to words of disrespect. This doesn't strike me as the time to take that chance."

"Remember, I was against hiring him."

"Not enough against it to refuse to pay him your assessment, I hear."

Bill whimpered brokenly, "That's right. The fear of sudden death has the same shape to all of us, Perfessor. I wish we could find us a meaner, faster gunman somewhere, but I see two reasons why that wouldn't work so well either. In the first place, I doubt there is anybody meaner and faster. Second place, we'd just have him on our backs instead of Dewey Score."

"How about Mr. Cahoon?" Beansie gulped. "I know he don't want the job, but he sure could put that Dewey Score in his place in a hurry."

"His name did come up, yes it did," Bill said, "but it just don't seem sensible to me somehow. He never struck me as much of a gunman, and yet—and yet—"

"If you could get him to do it, Mr. Shenker, he could do it like falling off'n a wet log."

Bill looked hopelessly down at the ground and then up into Beansie's eyes. "I wonder how much he'd want for the job though. We'd be even worse off if he wanted more money than Dewey Score does."

"You're not serious, are you?" said the Perfessor.

"About what?"

"About Honker Cahoon being a gunman."

"Well, the talk is that he's the best there is."

Blythe waved his arm impatiently. "Oh, sure, but whose talk, his? He's a deadly man with words, I grant you that, but who has ever seen him in action?"

"I have!" Beansie said fiercely.

Blythe peered at him through his glasses with a smile. "Against whom?"

"Against two of the worst gunmen anywhere in the whole natural world, Lou Burnside and Merle Watson. And he let them get him between them first, and he just didn't care! When he got ready he just sent them on their way like a couple of wet cats."

"You *saw* this yourself?" Blythe said, perplexed.

"Yes. They really did get out of there, and he didn't even have to draw on them. They knowed better than to let it go that far."

Blythe looked at Bill. "Maybe we have misjudged our honking friend. It might be a good idea for you to have a little talk with him."

"I dunno, I seem to bring out the worst in him. Every time he opens his mouth, it costs me money."

"Sometimes we have to choose between money and peace of mind—money and self-respect—money and life itself, Bill."

"Don't push me!" Bill shouted. He cringed and looked around fearfully, then went on in a lower tone of voice: "Let me think about it. Everything's so dad-blamed simple to you, Perfessor."

"Yes. I have only my life to lose."

Beansie remembered his errand. He started on up the street, and then suddenly reined in again. One look, and he kicked his horse between two tents and waited. When nothing happened he dismounted and peered around one of the tents.

A hundred yards away a rider had stopped to speak to a man on the street. He rode a magnificent bay horse with four white feet and a white face, a horse that would stand out boldly anywhere. The man himself was dressed entirely in brown. He was very tall, with good shoulders and big hands, and the very way he sat his fine horse showed that he was used to courtesy, if not downright deference, wherever he rode.

Beansie could not see his face clearly, under his expensive, flat-crowned brown Stetson. He stood holding his horse's reins until the stranger thanked the man on the street and began walking his horse closer. Beansie moved his own horse around behind the tent, keeping it between himself and the big man.

He got a glimpse of an unhappy face with sad blue eyes and a turned-down mouth, and he closed his own eyes and heaved a great sigh. He waited, hidden behind the tent, for a long time. When he started back to the cabin, he walked along behind the tents, one tent at a time, until he was close to the timber. Not until then did he mount and shake his horse into a hard run.

It seemed to Honker that Beansie was quieter than usual as they headed for the Zigzag T. Again the sun came out and showed them a beautiful day when they reached the top of the ridge. By the time they started back with the cattle, the last of the fog had melted away.

Beansie seemed to come out of a faraway dream. He looked around as though seeing the beautiful valley of the Zigzag T for the first time.

"I bet Mr. Shenker is going to sell this place," he said.

"What of it?" said Honker.

95

"If I had money enough I'd buy it."

"If I had money enough to buy a steamboat, mebbe I'd buy one of them too."

"I bet I know how you could get enough money, Mr. Cahoon."

Honker turned on him savagely. "If you mean set up in business as a town marshal in Camp Corinth, forget it. I ain't going to, and that's that."

"Then how do you plan for us to get rich?"

"You'll see."

"Are you just showing consideration for Dewey Score for the sake of old times?"

"Beansie, I wouldn't show him no consideration at all, for no reason whatsoever. I just ain't going to take none of that riffraff that serious. They leave me alone, I'll leave them alone."

"Every man for himself, you mean."

Honker merely shrugged. They rode on a way, and then Beansie tried again, keeping one sharp eye on Honker's grim expression.

"Mr. Cahoon, you ever hear of a famous gunman by the name of Worried Smith?"

No answer. Honker, if anything, looked angrier than ever.

"He was one of the old-timers, sir. They say that they don't make them like him any more. They say that if he hadn't give up the gunman's life, you wouldn't hear anything about people like Dewey Score and Lou Burnside and Merle Watson and the like."

Still no answer. They rode on awhile in silence, and then Beansie said, "He was a famous train robber in his time. He retired from that and turned over a new leaf and hung up his guns for good. They called him Worried Smith because of his worried expression."

Honker turned an amber wolf's eye on the boy. "Is he another one of your heroes?"

"Criminy, no! When a man reforms, you can't hardly call him a hero no more, can you?"

"I was just going to say that if he was a hero of yourn, you might be interested in a little visit I had with him."

"Gee whackers, I sure would! Did you know him?"

"I would have to say I did, yes. In fact, I reckon it was me that caused him to give up train robbing as a trade. Look, son, them steers has settled down to gaze, so let's let them, and I'll tell you about this here little experience of mine. Shoot, though, it really wasn't much. It was down there on the International and Great Northern, in a day coach. The I.G.N. was held up so often in them days, you always changed your money into paper bills and put them in your boot, before you bought your ticket—"

The creative fire had leaped into full blaze in Honker. Gone was his expression of suicidal despair, and along with it, the insoluble problem caused by the presence of Dewey Score in Camp Corinth. Like a drinking man fallen off the wagon, Honker was happy again while it lasted. He threw his leg around the horn of his saddle and told Beansie about it.

He was riding a day coach that was kind of crowded that time, setting there next to the window with his hat across his face, catching himself a little *siesta*. The seat next to him was empty, but after the train stopped at this little station, a man got in and sat down beside him. Honker didn't pay him no attention at all until the conductor came through, taking up tickets.

"I didn't have time to buy me no ticket, so I'll have to pay cash fare," this fella beside Honker said. "I only want to go to the next stop, Agua Amarga. How much is it to there?"

"It's only thirty-two cents," the conductor said, "but I can't believe you want to go there. Ain't nothing there but a sidetrack and a section house, not even a depot. You sure don't want to get off at Agua Amarga."

The man said yes he did, and he handed the conductor half a dollar and got back his eighteen cents change. The conductor moved on, and then the man tapped Honker on the arm very politely. Honker looked around, and that was when he noticed how worried this man looked.

"Excuse me, but I wonder if I could ask you to change seats with me?" he said. "I would like to set there by the window, if you don't mind, until we get to Agua Amarga, and then you can have your seat back."

"Why no, I don't mind," Honker said.

He got up and changed seats, and this other man pressed his worried face up against the glass. What he wanted to do was see as far ahead of the train as possible when it went around a curve.

Honker knowed then what was up, because then he recognized this man as Worried Smith, the famous gunman and train robber with the meanest gang of outlaws in the natural world. Sure as the dickens, there was going to be a train robbery at Agua Amarga!

The gang leader's job was to get on the train and buy his fare to Agua Amarga, so the train would have to stop there to let him off. His gang would wait at Agua Amarga with the horses. After the train and all the passengers had been robbed, they'd put out the fire in the engine so the train couldn't move until a new one was built. By then they'd be long gone and unheard of.

Honker lay back in his seat and pulled his hat over his face and put his boots up on the back of the seat in front of them. Just then the train whistled for the next stop, and the conductor stuck his head in at the door from the vestibule and called the name of the town.

"Agua Amarga! Agua Amarga, all out for anybody getting off at Agua Amarga."

This man with the worried face stood up and tapped Honker on the arm. "Excuse me," he said.

Honker went right on pretending to nap. The stranger tapped him again, a little harder.

"This is my station coming up," he said, "and you've got me fenced in," he said.

Honker took his hat off his face. "Yes sir," he said, "it appears I sure have, Mr. Smith."

"Oh. I see you know me."

"Yes, I know you, and I know what you plan to do."

"You do? Then my advice to you is don't butt in, and move your big feet."

"No," said Honker, "I'll just move my hand instead. I like to be acquainted with my traveling companions, and I like them to know me, so I'll be glad to shake your hand. My name is Wilber W. Cahoon, sometimes referred to as Honker, and if you would ruther draw your weapon than shake hands with me—why, go ahead, start the festivities!"

"Just my luck to run into you at such a time," said Worried Smith, looking more worried than ever. "Listen, Cahoon, fair is fair. I don't butt into your business, do I? Then why do you butt into mine?"

"I'll tell you why," Honker said. "This is just a blamed

nuisance, the outrageous way you do things. You stall a train as much as two or three hours, and I've got to keep an important appointment tonight, which I'll miss if I permit you to get away with this foolishness. So you just forget about robbing this train, and wait for some other one."

Worried's hand started toward the butt of his gun, and he said, "If you force me to do this, we're both going to be very sorry. Why, this is point-blank range! We would just shoot each other to death, that's all, and you don't gain anything by that."

"There you are making another mistake, friend," Honker said, "because I don't have no plans at all to get shot. If you want to get off at Agua Amarga with no teeth, and holding your gun in your gums, start your festivities."

"This is pretty raw of you, when I was as civil to you as I was," Worried complained.

Just then the conductor came back into the car, yelling, "Where's the party that wanted out at Agua Amarga? Next stop coming up, Agua Amarga."

Honker whistled him over and said, "My friend has done changed his mind. He wants to go on through to your next flag stop."

"To Sam Vance Junction?" said the conductor. "He don't want to go there. That's a worse hellhole than Agua Amarga. There is nothing there but a sidetrack and a lot of prairie-dog holes."

"That's where he wants to go, Sam Vance Junction."

"That will be forty-one cents then."

Honker looked at Worried Smith and said, "Pay him forty-one cents like he told you."

"I haven't got it," Worried Smith said. "All I got left is

eighteen cents change from the four bits I paid him to get to Agua Amarga."

"I'll tell you what I'm going to do, Mr. Smith. I'm going to stake you to a dollar, and you can pay me back the next time we meet."

"You can well believe I'll pay you back," Worried Smith said, "but not the way you think."

Honker gave the conductor a dollar, and the conductor gave Worried Smith fifty-nine cents in change and then leaned out of the window to wave the engineer not to stop at Agua Amarga. Worried Smith pressed his face against the glass until they almost got to Agua Amarga. Honker could see several rough-looking cowboys running around and waving their arms at the train, and Worried pulled his face back fast. In a minute the place was behind them.

"Honker," said Worried, "you haven't got one drop of human compassion in your whole entire make-up, have you? My boys will kill me when they catch me."

"If I was you," said Honker, "I wouldn't let them catch me. I'd get me a horse in Sam Vance Junction, and I wouldn't be too particular how I got it or whose it was. And I'd head for Indian territory so fast all anybody would see would be a tunnel of dust with me and the horse at the end of it."

"What a thing to happen to me!" Worried said. "Why, I'll never live this down!"

It was one of the finest dreams Honker had ever lived, and he could not be blamed for a sharp twinge of regret when it ended. Beansie expelled his pent-up breath in a long, quivering sigh.

"Well gee for whackers, so that's how Worried Smith hauled off and turned honest, is it?" he said.

"Not entirely honest," said Honker. "He never did pay me back that dollar, but of course we never did run into each other again."

Strangely enough, this time Honker did not suffer the tortures of conscience afterward. His buoyant mood survived, even after one of the steers got away when they were running them into the corral and it took them an extra twenty minutes to finish the job. He did not even scold Beansie when the boy lost his temper at the mice as he was putting the bowls of beans on the table. As for Beansie, he could even put up with the mice, to have Mr. Cahoon contented again.

CHAPTER NINE

For the next six days they did not leave the cabin except to go to the Zigzag T for more cattle. To the boy it was a completely happy time. Mr. Cahoon did not have much to say, but he seemed gentle and relaxed. He ate what Beansie put in front of him, and napped a great deal. They did not talk much. Several times Beansie tried to draw Honker out about his experiences as a gunman among other gunmen, but he did not rise to the bait.

Early on the morning of the seventh day Beansie stepped out of the cabin to see a handsome young buck deer just beyond the corral. The deer did not see him as it picked its dainty way back into the timber. The boy left the door open while he got his .30-30. Mr. Cahoon was still asleep, but there was a pot of coffee on the stove in case he woke up before the boy got back.

It took Beansie only a half-hour to stalk the deer and bring it down with one shot. It was too heavy for him to carry, so he returned to the cabin for his horse. He did not go in, but it was pretty clear that Mr. Cahoon was still sleeping. He saddled the horse and led it to where he had left the deer.

Getting the deer up across the horse's back took some doing, but he made it. He started back to the cabin, leading his horse with his left hand and carrying the .30-30 in his right.

He was almost in sight of the cabin when he heard someone shouting:

"Hi, there. Hi, the cabin! Anybody to home?"

The voice was familiar. Beansie tied the horse and slipped forward between the trees, carrying the carbine at the ready.

Dewey Score sat his horse in the clearing just beyond the cabin. As Beansie watched, the cabin door opened and Honker Cahoon came out in his sock feet, yawning and stretching sleepily. Beansie dropped to his knee and cocked the carbine as quietly as he could.

"What's all the hollering about?" Honker demanded in his foghorn voice. "What do you mean, coming here and waking decent people up out of a sound sleep?"

Score's frock coat was unbuttoned to expose his two guns and his crossed cartridge belts, but he raised both hands to show his peaceful intentions.

"I reckon you're Honker Cahoon."

"You reckon right."

"I don't have to tell you that I'm Dewey Score. Everybody knows Dewey Score."

"Oh, you don't say."

"Now dad-blame it, Cahoon, you don't need to start out by being so dad-blamed sarcastic. I come here to have a little friendly talk with you, with my hands in the air out of respect to your murderous reputation, and you stand there and make fun of me."

"Go ahead, then, talk away."

"Why can't I tie my horse and come inside? I don't call this very sociable of you, Cahoon, by golly, I don't! Seems to me I smell coffee. I'll hang my weapons on my saddle horn and come in defenseless as a naked, newborn babe, and over a cup of coffee let's talk over a few things."

"I can use a cup of coffee myself. All right, come inside, I ain't p'ticular."

Beansie kept the .30-30 trained on Score until the gunman had taken off both guns, buckled the buckles of the holster belts, and draped them over the saddle horn. Then he tied his horse to the corral fence and went to the cabin door.

"After you," he said, bowing to Honker.

"After you," said Honker.

"I beg you, sir—go ahead!"

"If you're scared to turn your back on me," said Honker, "I'll show you I ain't scared to turn mine on you."

Honker went into the cabin. Score followed him. The door closed. Beansie crept as close as he dared, to where he could hear the deep, baritone rumble of their conversation without making out any of the words. He did not trust Dewey Score at all. It would be like him to carry a little pocket gun. He might get away with killing Mr. Cahoon. But if he did, Beansie meant to see that he did not leave here alive.

This had been a strange time for Honker. There was no letup in his feeling of being cornered by fate. One of these days he would hear from Smoky O'Neill, and his chance to get rich might arrive. That it would mean facing the future in Camp Corinth was never far from his mind. He was torn between his cowardice and his avarice as never before in his life, and yet he had not been unhappy.

That tale he had unfolded to Beansie, about the forced reformation of Worried Smith at his hands, had been a watershed in his state of mind. Like a drunkard gone back to his drink, after a virtuous period of abstinence, Honker had again taken refuge in his dream world. And this time there was a strange feeling of reality to it.

When a liar comes to the point of believing his own lies, they come very close to being the truth. Honker, these last few days, had been—at least in his own mind—a character so entrancing that it was hard to lay it aside for grim, unromantic reality. He was The Old Gunnie, the badman who had met and bested the worst of them and then let his guns go silent for lack of competition. He was a male Nemesis retired, the hero in eclipse, the last survivor of a giant race.

It was The Old Gunnie whose pleasant calm had made Beansie feel so good. It was The Old Gunnie who slept so well, ate so appreciatively whatever Beansie cooked, and then sat with his feet up in the sun, a smile on his scarred and swarthy face, and a dreamy, faraway look in his amber wolf's eyes. It was The Old Gunnie who lived each moment as it came, as Honker Cahoon never had been able to do, unafraid of the future, tolerant of the present, and at last forgiving of the past.

It was still The Old Gunnie who opened the door and stamped into the cabin with Dewey Score at his back; but as the door closed behind him and he turned and faced the notorious badman for the first time, the fictitious serendipity in him began to seep away. They stood in silence a moment, studying each other narrowly. It was Score who spoke first.

"I hung my guns up, Cahoon. I'd take it a sight friendlier, sir, if you wasn't armed," he said.

It was The Old Gunnie who unbuckled his gun belt, wrapped it around the .45, and pitched it across the room, on top of Beansie's bunk. It was still The Old Gunnie who said honkingly, in a voice that made the lamp chimney vibrate on the shelf behind the stove, "Suit you? Or you want me to tie one hand behind my back, too?"

Score made a gesture of appeal with both empty hands. "Now, Cahoon, why've you got a chip on your danged shoulder for? Why can't we set down and have a friendly talk, like a man and his guest ort to?"

"Set down," said Honker. "How do you take your coffee?"

"Black."

"Same here."

Honker clattered two mugs to the table and picked up the dishrag to hold the hot handle of the coffeepot. He poured both mugs full and sat down across from Score. Their eyes met, and Honker suddenly felt quite a bit less like The Old Gunnie.

"You make mighty good coffee, Cahoon."

Honker acknowledged the compliment with a surly grunt.

"Yes sir," Score went on in a voice grown somehow oily, "a man could ride a fur piece and wear out a stout horse and not come onto coffee half this good."

"You didn't come here to say polite things about our coffee. What's on your mind?" Honker burst out.

He saw Score wince from the catamount snarl in his voice and misunderstood. What was sheer raw nerves in the gunman, Honker took for an expression of disdain. His own nerves were suddenly vibrating painfully.

"You like to go right for the throat of a problem, I see," Score said, "and that's the way I like to do business, so I'll just lay it out with every card face up. I'm the town marshal of Camp Corinth, but you prob'ly already heard that."

Honker nodded. "Somebody said that, yes."

"Supposed to pay five hundred dollars a month. That sounded like a lot of money to me when I ran for the job, as you might say. But, Cahoon, that is just penny ante in that town. There's millions being made there. And here I am, prob'ly the fastest gunman in the world, working for that kind of a penny-ante price."

Honker did not utter a sound, but his yellow eyes had narrowed, and the odd scar on his face had become a little more noticeable. Uncompromising reality was at last dawning in him. Across the table sat a man of legendary reputation, a towering myth become flesh and blood, calmly confessing himself the fastest gunman in the world. Inside Honker's porous soul, the specter of The Old Gunnie began looking around for an escape route, and found millions of ways out, all ignoble.

"It don't stand to reason for a man of my quality to work for wages, any more than it does for you," Score went on. "You and me are too good for a plain low-down job, Cahoon. I wouldn't fool around with this town marshal's job five minutes if it wasn't for one thing—you."

One of Honker's bushy black eyebrows rose. "Me?" he said in a terrible voice.

Score flinched. "Yes, if I's sure you and me was in agreement, we could carve this here situation up like it was a roasted Christmas goose. I don't know what kind of a dodge you've got working on this old thief of a Bill Shenker, but I ain't interfering in it. In fact, I'd be proud to help it along if I could. Now, how can I be any fairer than that?

"All I ask of you is the same thing. I'm going to raise the ante on everybody beginning today. First I'm going to notify this old blister of a Bill Shenker that his bill goes up to *one hundred dollars a day!* Minute he gives in, it'll be easy to collect from five to ten dollars a day from everybody else. This job ort to be worth five hundred a *day*, Cahoon, not five hundred a month.

"All I want from you is the promise you'll stand aside and not take sides against me. This old Shenker robber must be taking in close to a thousand a day himself. He can afford it. Ain't no more than fair if he shares some of his ill-gotten gains around among respectable working people like you and me. That's how I look at it, Cahoon, and I bet you feel the same way in your heart.

"Next, I figger that you and me together ort to go over and have a talk with them people that's running that hard-rock mine. The talk I hear is, the color is thinning out pretty bad. They may be almost to the end of the silver deposit, or they may be just in a fault of some kind. One thing is sure, them managers is mighty worried right now. They're ready to listen to reason if you and me offer to protect them for—oh, how does two thousand dollars a week sound to you?"

"Protect them from what?" said Honker.

"Why, from everything. But why do you have to holler at me like that, Cahoon?"

Honker took it as a rebuke and did not reply. He had gone cold all over as the realization sank deeper within him that he sat face to face against the one and only Dewey Score. A figure out of his own fictitious past had come here to haunt him. It was bound to happen some-

time, he thought, but danged if this ain't the most in-
convenient time in the world. I got to hang on somehow
until I hear from Smoky. . . .

"Cahoon," Score said, "you and me could go out of
these mountains rich in just a few weeks. You *know* we
could. And yet I got a feeling you're against me. Am I
right?"

No answer, but Honker's Adam's apple worked in
mighty spasms. Score got a little pink in the face. His eyes
narrowed.

"You're against me, ain't you?" he whispered.

No answer.

Down came Score's hand on the table, palm down, in
a resounding slap.

"Here I am, unarmed. Well," he said, "you win this
trick. But dad-blamed if I haven't got a mind to call you
out. Let's see just which one of us is fastest on the draw.
Tell you what I'm gonna do, Cahoon. I'm gonna leave
here and get on my horse and leave my guns hanging on
the saddle horn until I'm plumb out of sight of your place.
And if you're half a man, you'll let me go and not shoot
me in the back.

"At noon, though, I'll be waiting in front of Bill
Shenker's Silverado with both of my guns on. If you have
got the guts, you put a gun on and come there and meet
me, man to man and face to face. Let's find out if you're
any better man than Ontario Slim was. I come here and
make you a fair and decent proposition, to divide everything fair and square, and how do you treat me? Why,
you set there a-sneering and a-hollering at me, like I was
dirt under your feet—"

His mouth continued to work, but Honker had gone
stone-deaf. The scar on his face stood out pallidly against

his swarthy skin as abject terror took possession of him. He looked death in the eye, and as usual when this happened, his strident, overbearing voice went out of control, and he said that which even The Old Gunnie, at his best, would never have dared to say.

Beansie, squatting with his back against a tall sugar pine, the .30-30 at the ready, had grown more and more nervous as the two men chatted inside the cabin. The more he thought of it, the less he liked Mr. Cahoon's situation, locked in there with that double-crossing Dewey Score. He was just about to come to a decision to tiptoe up to the window and cover Score, just in case, when the familiar rumble, which even stout log walls could not muffle, came to his ears:

"Oh, who do you think you are, talking to me like that? You make me sick and tired, that's what you do, with your talk. Why, Bill Shenker's a friend of mine, and who are you to proposition me to rob my own friend? And I ain't going to meet you at noon in no showdown, either, because that kind of show-off shooting just makes me plumb tired. I hope you don't think I would take something like that serious, from riffraff like you," Honker said.

"Instead of meeting you like that, at noon, what I say we're going to do is this, Dewey Score: You just get on your horse and ride straight on out of here, and don't you even put your guns back on when you get to Camp Corinth, because if I hear about it, I'm going to have to come after you and box your dad-blamed ears for you. I have just completely lost patience with you, that's what I did!

"I let you come into a decent cabin, and I give you a

cup of coffee, and I set down and try to treat you like a
human being, and you have got the gall to make me that
kind of a proposition! Well sir, Mr. Dewey Score, I just
don't care for that a bit, no indeedy! I just despise anybody that abuses my hospitality that way, and in fact I
can't stand the sight of you a minute longer, so I give you
just half a minute to get on your horse and get out of here
and do like I tell you."

He certainly is a great man, Beansie thought, listening
to the rumble of that prophet's voice. He was even
surer of Honker's greatness when Dewey Score came out
of the cabin with the skirts of his coat flying. He was so
furious he was red-faced, and his hands were clenched
into fists. He untied his horse, swung up into the saddle,
and spun the horse to face the cabin.

"You in there. Cahoon!" he shouted. "I dare you to
meet me at noon like I said. I dare you!"

He whirled the horse and was gone in a gallop. Beansie
waited until he was out of sight, and then went into the
cabin. As he entered he carefully lowered the hammer
of the .30-30.

Honker heard the click—the first sound to penetrate
his deafness. He turned, startled, with a look of such
ferocity that Beansie shrank back against the wall like a
bearskin nailed to it.

"I-I-I'm sorry, I didn't think," the boy stammered.

Honker's eyes rolled wildly. He tried several times to
pick up his coffee cup but could not. Beansie leaped to
pick it up for him.

"This is cold, Mr. Cahoon, sir. I'll get you some fresh,"
he said. "Say, you sure did put that Dewey Score in his
place, didn't you?"

Honker took the scalding coffee and managed to get

a few swallows down. The tears came to his eyes. He had no hope of living much past noon. When he failed to show up in front of the Silverado, Score would come out here and shoot him down like a chicken-killing dog.

Beansie brought his buck to the cabin and began to dress it. His mind plainly was not on his work. He was so anxious to get to Camp Corinth and see the fun that he was mangling the deer badly. Honker, who was just as anxious to know what was going on in camp, finally sent him on his way.

"I'll do the dad-blamed work myself," he growled, taking the butcher knife.

Beansie leaped on his horse and was gone.

Time passed, and Dewey Score did not come to gun Honker down like a cowardly dog in hiding. Another hour passed before a shining-eyed boy showed up at the cabin with a wondrous tale to tell.

Seemed Dewey had pulled up in front of the Silverado and hollered for Bill Shenker to come out. Bill was afraid to go and afraid to stay, but he went at last. And there, Dewey Score sat his horse, his eyes full of a sick and frustrated fury, both his holstered guns hanging from his saddle horn.

Dewey gathered saliva in his mouth and with a look of infinite scorn spat copiously on the ground between him and Bill.

"And that," he said, "is what I think of you, Bill Shenker! That goes for your whole town too. You hire a cold-blooded murderer like Honker Cahoon, and all I can say is, This is just what I'd expect from a cold-blooded rich man like you. And I'll tell you something else too."

Dewey stood up and pointed an accusing finger at Bill. "I hope I never see you or your dirty, muddy old mosquito-ridden Camp Corinth again as long as I live, and you just try to make me change my mind. Just try!" he shouted.

He spun his horse and was gone at a gallop, down the muddy wagon road to the Mokelumne and the outside world, his deadly guns still hanging on his saddle horn. And Bill Shenker took off his hat and ran his fingers wildly through his hair. He stumbled slightly as he went back into the Silverado. When he came out that evening in his bull wagon for his day's beef, he was so polite to Honker, he just about made Beansie sick at his stomach.

Honker took it with dignity. The Old Gunnie had come home.

CHAPTER TEN

Up the same muddy wagon road the next morning came a ramshackle wagon drawn by four tough little broncs. The wagon was covered with dark, weather-stained canvas that looked very much like a folded tent. In any case, it effectively hid whatever was under it. On the seat of the wagon was a knotty, wiry, tough-looking little man with merry blue eyes and a gnarled face that could have been carved out of a potato.

"Anybody know where I'd find Honker Cahoon?" he called out. "Aye, where's me ould friend, Honker? Go tell him, somebody, that Smoky O'Neill is here."

Word reached Bill Shenker promptly—as all word did in Camp Corinth. It was well known that he did not invite strangers to hang around his meat camp in the clearing in the timber. Bill walked out into the middle of the street to meet the wagon.

"Whoa, whoa, 'tis harder to stop yez than it is to get yez started!" the wagon driver shouted to his horses in a cheerful Irish brogue. He grinned at Bill Shenker. "Like a good boy, why don't yez earn a quarter and go tell me friend Honker Cahoon that myself is here?"

"Keep your quarter," Bill said coldly. "What do you want with him? What's in the wagon there? That looks like a tent. You aim to start up in business here? What kind of business? Honker works for me, you know, and I don't like to have him bothered during working hours."

The Irishman put his finger to his lips. "Aha, then you'd be the stingy rich man he mentioned in his letter, belike. I wouldn't keep him from his work. Where would I find him?"

"You ain't answered my questions yet."

"No, and I don't plan to. Now be a good lad and tell me where's me friend Honker Cahoon."

Bill remembered in time that only yesterday Honker had driven the famous Dewey Score out of town. Something still did not make sense, but Bill's instincts were conservative, and they told him now that this was not the time to risk offending Honker. Reluctantly he pointed down the road to where it entered the timber.

"Yonder a piece, to where there's a cabin and a corral in a clearing by the creek," he said, "but if you tie up there for the night, I'll have to charge you rent. And feed for your teams will be extra."

"Put it on Honker's bill," Smoky O'Neill said with a wink. "We're partners, ye know. What's his is mine and what's mine is his."

O'Neill whistled to his team, and the wagon vanished in the timber. When he reached the clearing, O'Neill found no one at home. He tied his teams to the wagon and went into the cabin. He took one good look around and went back out to the wagon to bring in part of his supplies.

Honker and Beansie had gone over to the Zigzag T that morning for more cattle. They arrived back early in the afternoon, to see strange horses tied to a strange wagon, and smoke coming from the cabin chimney. Honker's dark face lighted up like a sunrise.

"Smoky! I bet Smoky O'Neill is here!" he said. "Put

up the horses, boy, and wait outside till you're called."

He slid from his horse and hurried into the cabin. Beansie's curiosity about Smoky O'Neill and his wagon was as great as Bill Shenker's, and was no better satisfied. It was almost an hour before he was called to dinner.

And what a dinner! Smoky had brought provisions up from Sacramento and was as inventive a cook as he was an electrician. Beansie had left venison to stew on the stove when they left for the Zigzag T that morning. Now there were dumplings in a rich gravy such as can be made only with good venison. There were potatoes fried with onions and some mushrooms that Smoky had picked while resting his teams on the wagon road that morning, and blackberry cobbler to top it off.

It was almost irreverent, to Beansie, to see the way Honker shoveled in the food. His mind was a thousand miles away, and he might as well have been eating pine nuts. Honker and Smoky had done all the talking necessary, and Beansie's curiosity still went unsatisfied.

"I noticed a nice empty place straight across the road from the Silverado," Smoky said when Honker at last finished eating. "That seems to me to be the best lot for our purposes. I've a bit of work I want to do on the outfit, and our signs to paint and all. If you'll take the boy and get the lot ready for our tent and cut a center pole for it, we can start setting up tomorrow morning."

"Across from the Silverado," Honker said. "That ain't going to make Bill Shenker very happy, but you're right, it's the best place."

"By far!" Smoky said cheerfully. "He's not going to be overjoyed wherever we stake down."

Honker stood up. "All right, let me have your shovel, and I'll take Beansie and get at it."

"I brought no shovel. I had trouble making the money go as far as it did. There should be plenty of shovels in a mining camp, Honker."

"There ain't never plenty of shovels in a mining camp. You could buy a gold-plated shovel cheaper and easier in Sacramento than you could a plain one here."

"Just so you get the lot leveled off, one way or another," Smoky said indifferently.

As Honker and Beansie rode into camp together, Honker said, "Now that's just like Smoky. Smartest man I ever knowed, and yet I bet there ain't another man in California that would come up to a mining camp without bringing his own shovel."

"Is he the man that's going to make us rich?" Beansie asked.

"Yes. All his life his idees has had to go to waste because he never had the money to turn them into any kind of a working business. You and me, Beansie, are the capitalists of this here venture. Smoky hasn't got a dime left of the money I sent him, and it's going to take every gold piece we got to bankroll this deal."

"If you say so, I reckon it's all right," Beansie said, dubiously. "Only—"

"Only what?"

"Smoky seems like such a cheerful old joker, and you always said it took a mean man to make money."

For an instant Honker's face showed his dismay. "Mebbe Smoky is the one cheerful man in the whole world that can get rich," he said then. "Mebbe he'll get meaner when they start handing over the gold pieces to us. And mebbe this is just another pipe dream and we'll all go out of here broke, like poor men usually do."

"I reckon there's risk to any money-making scheme."

"We're sure going to find out. How much money have we got between us, Beansie?"

"We been here thirteen days, and I still got all Bill paid us. When he pays us tonight, I'll have a hundred and forty dollars."

"I got that much too, and fifty dollars left over from what I brung in. Smoky says we ort to have five hundred to start with, but he claims we can make do with less." Honker took his hat off and mopped the nervous sweat from his forehead. "It has got to be enough—it has just *got* to!"

Beansie studied him. "Mr. Cahoon, are you getting cold feet about this proposition of getting rich? Because if you are, whatever you decide is all right with me."

Honker turned on him furiously. "Why, are *you* getting cold feet?"

"No, but—"

"Then drop it! This is so new to me, I don't trust my own judgment. I'm scared to death I'll lose heart and slip away while Smoky's back is turned. It ain't that I'm scared of losing my money. I been broke often enough before."

His amber eyes narrowed malevolently as he glared at Beansie. "I reckon that what I'm afraid of is getting rich. It's too big a change, boy! When you get to my age, you want things to sort of slide along the same old way, day after day."

"Not at my age, Mr. Cahoon. I ain't a bit scared of changing to be rich instead of poor."

"All right, you keep me from backsliding. You see that I don't lose my nerve and let Smoky O'Neill down."

They had arrived at the vacant lot across the "street" from Bill Shenker's Silverado. Even Beansie knew enough to realize that it needed considerable leveling if a tent were to be put up here. An hour's tent-by-tent inquiry failed to turn up a shovel anywhere. Even Bill Shenker had none.

They were about to ride out to Stairsteps, where Honker hoped to borrow a shovel from the mine syndicate for a few hours, when the Perfessor, Judson Blythe, caught up with them. For once he was stone sober.

"Understand you're looking for a shovel, Honker," he said.

"Yes," Honker said sourly, "and you're the last man I'd ask for one, because you never yet got that close to hard work."

"As it happens, I do have a shovel for sale however."

"You do? How much do you want for it?"

"Thirty dollars."

"Thirty dollars for a shovel?" Honker howled. "I'll get down and scratch it out with my fingers before I'll pay that much for a dad-blamed shovel."

"Twenty then?"

Honker looked at the empty lot. "All right, if it's in good shape."

"It's not a new shovel, of course, but you'll find it has been remarkably preserved by a generous coating of ferric oxide. In fact, Honker, I guarantee that it has more ferric oxide on it than any shovel in Camp Corinth."

"We don't need no fancy stuff, just a good working shovel."

"Pay in advance. That's the rule in any mining camp, Honker. The shovel is under my bedroll, in my tent yonder. Ah, thank you! And now, if you'll excuse me, I'm a little late for my morning stimulant. Devil of an inconvenience, Honker, being broke."

Blythe took his twenty-dollar gold piece and almost ran to the Silverado. Honker and Beansie located his ragged tent and found the shovel under his bedroll, as promised. It was surely the oldest shovel in the entire Fat Tree Creek mining area.

The handle had been replaced countless times, most recently by a springy length of green wood. The blade had been worn to no more than half its original length and was so rusty it was inconceivable that it could be driven into the ground. Honker almost wept with mortification, but it was indubitably a shovel, and they could work with it.

In a few hours they had the lot leveled. "But I'll get even with him if it's the last thing on earth I do," Honker vowed as they rode homeward.

They found Smoky O'Neill sitting in the sunlight beside the corral, peacefully smoking his pipe. He shook his head as they approached. "Can't go inside just yet," he said. "I just set the trap again. It fills up in about thirty minutes. I've already got about thirty of the little beggars."

They dismounted. Honker brandished the shovel at Smoky. "We're off to a good start. Did you ever run into a fella by the name of Judson Blythe anywhere? Mostly he's called Perfessor."

"Oh, to be sure. One of the most brilliant men I ever met," said Smoky.

"And the crookedest. Look at the shovel he sold us for twenty dollars. What was that stuff he said he had it coated with, Beansie?"

"Something like ferric oxide," said Beansie.

"Then he didn't cheat you at all," Smoky said with his infectious chuckle, "because ferric oxide is the chemical name for plain old iron rust. Honker, we can use this man in our business."

"How long is it going to take to set up?"

"No more than a couple of hours. We can be open by nightfall and by midnight can be a thousand dollars richer."

"A thousand dollars! How much is that, split three ways?"

"Three hundred and thirty-three dollars and thirty-three cents each."

Honker almost choked. "For only one night?"

"It could be a great deal more than that."

"Or less," Beansie ventured to say.

"Or less!" Smoky chuckled again. Then his knotty little face became serious. "No, I'm not going to believe that. All me life I have been the victim of poverty that prevented the exploitation of me own ideas. Now, bedad, I mean not to be the victim of me own fears. Rich we shall all be, and ye have the word of Smoky O'Neill on it."

"What will you do with your money when you get rich, Mr. O'Neill?" Beansie asked.

"A house big enough for me family, money in the bloody bank to buy potaties and ham for me table, and a new pair of shoes for me feet whenever I need them. What else could I aspire to at the age of me? Now you're different, lad. What will you do with your share?"

"Buy the Zigzag T if I can."

"And if you can't?"

"Some other cow ranch."

Honker and Smoky exchanged glances over the boy's head. "To prove, belike, that no man is the master of ye, is that right, lad?" Smoky said softly.

"Yes."

"Listen, Beansie, and learn something the aisy way that I had to learn the hard. We're niver intirely free. If we're not in bondage to someone, we're—why, we're like old Honker here, the loneliest man I've ever known."

"Not me!" Beansie's voice was shrill but positive.

"Have ye no family ties a-tall, a-tall? Is there nobody that cares about ye anywhere, boy?"

Beansie merely shook his head. Smoky watched him a moment and then jumped to his feet. "Very well, me trap must be full again. Hook up me team, please, and turn them around. I'm all right on a straight road but the worst coachman in the world on a turnabout. Let's be at setting up our money-making machine," he cried.

In ten minutes they were ready to head back to Camp Corinth. Last of all, Smoky came out of the house carrying a big wire cage in which forty-one mice raced and fought and kept up a continuous chattering and squeaking. Smoky set it tenderly on top of the load and sat down where he could hold it. Honker and Beansie got into the seat of the wagon, and Honker took the lines.

A crowd quickly collected when they pulled up across from the Silverado and started setting up their tent. It was not as big as the Silverado tent, by far, but it was a huge one. It had certainly seen better days and would be of little benefit once the heavy high-altitude snows of winter hit here.

"But we'll be long gone with our gold, and them as wants the tent can have it, fer all of me," said Smoky. "A hundred men can stand inside it without crowding, and a hundred and fifty if they'll put up with a bit of stepping on each other's boots. In that number, lad, there's a fortune for all of us."

Under the tent, the wagon had carried a strange assort-
ment of crates and boxes and planks. These Smoky
quickly assembled into a sort of flat-topped cabinet
about five feet wide and eight long. On the shelves under
the top of the cabinet, he put row after row of big crock-
ery jars, into which he poured chemicals from sundry
bags and bottles. Into each jar went a strangely shaped
piece of metal from which short wires ran to connect
with a single longer wire.

"The dear mysteries of electricity," Smoky crooned as
he deftly twisted wires together into some sort of pat-
tern known only to himself. "This will be, surely, the most
powerful circuit of galvanic batteries west of the
Rockies."

On top of the cabinet, he first spread a piece of brightly
painted oilcloth, with circles about a foot in diameter in
red. There were a dozen circles, each with a number—1
to 12—in the center. It reminded Beansie of the cover of
the craps table in the Silverado, except that this was
much simpler in design.

In the center of the table-like top of the cabinet,
Smoky assembled a glass box with sides about fifteen
inches high. The top was open. In the bottom, made of
wood, there were a dozen holes, each about an inch in
diameter.

No fewer than a hundred and fifty men had jammed
into the tent to watch these final preparations, and at
least that many more were fighting to get in. There was
still plenty of light outside, but it was growing dark in
the tent. Smoky left his electrical devices long enough to
hang two huge lanterns on the tent center pole, above
the cabinet table-top.

Beansie happened to glance at Honker Cahoon as these

preparations were under way. Honker looked so pallid that Beansie would not have been surprised to see him keel over in a faint. And indeed, Honker was thinking, There's no backing out now. It's now or never. Oh dear, is it worth all the worry, just to be rich . . . ?

Last of all, Smoky attached some queer-looking devices to the top of the glass walls of the box and then ran a strong silk cord from under the cabinet up to a small pulley on the center pole, from which it dangled loosely. Above the table, Smoky hung a big oilcloth sign:

GENUINE ELECTRIC MOUSE ROULETTE!

*The Latest Gaming Craze
of European Royalty, Now Here.*
Crowned Heads Of Old Country Love The Mice!

BET WHICH HOLE THE LITTLE MOUSIE PICKS!

All Bets Pay 5-1!
Start the Mouse Yourself!
Put Your Money On Your Favorite Number, Then Somebody Pulls The Cord! Hear The Thunder Crackle And Watch The Lightning Flash. Which Hole Will The Mousie Choose? He Must Force Open Spring-Loaded Trap Door To Escape Fury Of Violent ELECTRICAL STORM! Thrilling Way To Back Your Favorite Number—

ELECTRIC MOUSE ROULETTE!

CHAPTER ELEVEN

For what was probably the longest minute of Beansie's young life, it looked like total disaster. Not a sound came from the men who were packed so tightly into the tent that one more would have burst it. Smoky O'Neill, standing on his box behind the "mouse roulette" table, seemed to be holding his breath. He could have been a statue, so frozen was his stance.

Glancing up at Honker Cahoon beside him, Beansie saw a man who had aged thirty years in as many seconds. Honker's swarthy hide had gone gray. His face was flabby, senile, weak-looking. He had the stricken expression of a man who had staked his eating money on a bet that he had already lost.

Somehow Smoky found his voice. It was not much of a voice at first. His first words came out in a mousy squeak, but he had memorized this speech years and years ago, had dreamed of this moment time and time and again, and it came from deep in his mind with no conscious help on his part. Gradually his voice grew stronger:

"Make your bets, gentlemen, make your bets, and don't keep the mousies waiting! Mousie is ready to romp whenever you are, gents. Just put your money on the number of your choice, and then cheer your mousie home! The king and queen of Prussia, gentlemen, always bet the mousie with the whitest feet, and you'll excuse me I'm sure if I decline to say if he won or lost for them. Now the king of the Belgians, on the other hand, looked for a big, strong mousie with a fierce eye. My Lord the Duke of Gloucester wagered only on the lady mousies for odd numbers, and the males on even. Make your bets, gents, and watch the mousie scamper! Mousie will not move until there's money on the board."

"What mouse?" somebody called. "I don't see no mouse nowhere!"

"Ah, yes indeed, that's a good point. The first mouse is on the house, gents," said Smoky. "I'm a poet and didn't know it, right? First mouse is on the house. Very well, gentlemen, let's see what we get first!"

He held up the cage of mice and agitated it. There was a sharp click, and one mouse found himself trapped in a small screened cell in one corner. Smoky took the little cell out and shook the mouse out of it into the glass box on top of the table. He replaced the cell, put the cage down, and swung the rope that hung above it.

"A lusty big buck mouse, this one, gents. A real old he-mousie, tough and horny-handed! Put your bets down, gents, and then somebody pull the rope. Let's start the flow of the electric fluid and give this old buck mousie something to tell his grandchildren about. Remember, gents—we don't kill mousie, or do him any harm—no, sir. When he has had his little moment here with us, he's set free to return to his own society. Now look what I have in my hand, gentlemen. Gold—honest, minted, United States gold coins! Ready to pay off, gentlemen, when the electric mouse has had his little romp for your education, enjoyment, and profit. What hole will he choose, gentlemen? Pick your number and bet your pick, and watch mousie scramble!"

A tough-looking old miner whose face was so heavily covered with black beard that only his bright eyes and the tip of his red nose were visible pushed his way to the table. He flung two gold eagles down on it.

"Number six, that's my lucky number. Anybody likes another number better, you bet it, but I'll take six."

"Seven—seven for me!" someone in the rear of the crowd shouted. "I can't get through, dad-gum it. Put my ten-spot on seven before he spins it."

"Twelve! Double boxcars for me!"

"I'll bet the one spot. Twenty on the ace!"

"Can I get on six too? I'll bet six."

"You can bet every number if you like so long as there is space in the circle for your bet," Smoky said, his voice suddenly a rich, resonant baritone. "Hurry, hurry, hurry —get your bets down. The electric mouse is about to frolic, and the winner collects five to one."

"He ain't got but four hundred and ninety dollars to pay off with," Honker whispered to Beansie. "All I can say is, Lord guide that dad-blamed little varmint into a hole that won't break us."

"So this is why you didn't want me killing off no mice in the cabin," Beansie whispered back.

Honker nodded forlornly. "Yes. It seemed like such a crackin' good idee at the time. Now I wish you'd put out pizen instead."

Smoky's voice rose to a ringing shout.

"No more bets down, gents. The wagering is closed for this romp. Here, sir—you with the blue shirt and red suspenders—just give the rope a smart little tug, will you?"

The miner reached across somebody's shoulder to take the end of the rope. He pulled it sharply and then let go.

A gasp went up from the crowd as white lightning crackled back and forth between the bright rods attached to the tops of the glass walls. Buzzers buzzed, a clacker clacked, something sputtered like a rattlesnake with a cold in his rattles.

The mouse went crazy. Around and around the little glass box he raced, stopping first at this hole and then at the next. He tried 7 first, then 9, then 4, and then 1. He reversed direction, stopped at 5, reversed once more, tried 4 again. Finally he seemed to make up his mind—7, or bust.

Down into number 7 he went. There was a little click as the spring-loaded trap-door yielded, and he was gone.

"Number seven wins. The house pays four hundred and fifty dollars for the ninety bet!" Smoky droned. With his right hand he dribbled out the gold pieces, stacking them neatly on top of the bets already in the number 7 circle. Meanwhile his left hand slid over the table, gathering up the gold and bills on the losing numbers.

"Same mouse goes again, gents. Get your money down and stand by for the lightning flash. Mousie's baby mousies need new shoes, gentlemen! Mousie's dead game to try it again if you are. Be men or mice, gents. We take dollar bets too, you know, and they all pay five to one. Five dollars for every Liberty lady you tinkle down if old buck mousie picks the hole you bet."

Smoky O'Neill had suddenly undergone a total transformation of personality. His voice had become a hypnotic croupier's drone, with a touch that was more English than Irish in accent. His stubby fingers manipulated the coins deftly, and he stacked the currency with the deft fingertip skill of a bank teller.

The crowd responded by becoming silent and rapt, like betting crowds everywhere. Beansie felt Honker's hand close painfully around his upper arm. "That first bet cost us four hundred and fifty—near every cent Smoky had," he whispered in Beansie's ear, "but he pulled back over fourteen hundred from the other numbers. A thousand dollars profit right there!"

"That sure was a lucky mouse for us," Beansie whispered back.

"Yes. But I tell you what, we've cut it too fine. The crowd's not going to stand for only getting paid five to one when the odds are twelve to one."

As though Smoky had read his mind, his croupier's drone changed. He spoke a little faster and raised his voice to a slightly sharper and more penetrating timber:

"Tell you what, gents—in honor of the Czar of all the Rooshias, whose favorite game is electric mouse roulette, we're going to have a Rooshian double now. House will pay five to one on *two* numbers, not just one! How do you like this old buck mousie now, gentlemen? We'll pay five to one on the hole mousie chooses, as is our custom. And add the number three to that number, and the resulting number will also pay five to one! If mousie chooses a hole with a big number, so that the total is more than twelve, we simply start over. Thus, number eleven will pay five to one on eleven, and also five to one on two. Pay your respects to the Czar of all the Rooshias by betting for a Rooshian double, gents—two for the price of one!"

The crowd was silent again as it plunked down its money. The musical tinkle of gold coins, the rich slither of paper currency, with now and then the plebeian clang of silver dollars, were the only audible sounds.

Smoky reached under the table to retrieve the mouse from the cage into which it had fallen. He held it in his hand to drop it in the glass box. He swung the end of the rope for someone to catch, and someone caught it and gave it a sharp tug.

The lightning flashed, the buzzers buzzed, the clackers clacked. The frantic mouse raced back and forth, trying first one hole and then another. He gave up, finally, and huddled in the center of the box, doing nothing.

"Go on, you dirty little coward—run for it!" somebody shouted.

The shout aroused the mouse, which dashed from hole to hole while the crowd of miners whooped him on:

"Number seven—that's it, you miserable little varmint!"

"Try twelve again, damn you! You kin make it!"

"Go, mouse, go! Four or ten, either one. I'm on both four and ten, mouse. Look lively thar!"

"Nine, you numskull! Pshaw, you almost made it!"

The mouse vanished down number 8. "House pays five to one on number eight," Smoky droned, "and five to one on number eleven. Place your bets, gentlemen, while mousie rests and gets the electricity out of his system. Remember, gents, he has been galvanically charged while in the field of discharge, and his blood cells are temporarily upside down. Give him a moment to degalvanize while you place your bets. Five to one, gents, on the number of your own personal choice!"

Again the taut silence, except for the unforgettable symphony of gold, silver, and paper going down on the table in the numbered circles. Again Smoky reached under the table to take the mouse in his hand in full view of the audience.

"Pay no attention to all the marvels of galvanic batteries below, gents, because the area of discharge is inside the mousie's glass box," said Smoky. "He's fully degalvanized now and rarin' to go. Are your bets all down? Pull the rope, somebody, and hold it a moment this time. Give him a good, hard jolt—oh, it won't hurt him, it won't hurt him at all! But hey there, how he'll scamper!"

Scamper he did, before finding escape in number 2. Again Smoky left him there a moment to "degalvanize" while the gamblers got their bets down. Again he picked him up in his bare hand and put him in the box.

Six more times, in fact, did the mouse scamper before he quit and refused to play any more. The seventh time he merely huddled in the center of the glass box and refused to budge, though the crackle of lightning blinded them all.

"Put in a new mouse. You've plumb worn that one out," a miner shouted.

"Yes sir, we need a new mousie," said Smoky, "and under the rules, somebody is supposed to pay five dollars for the new one." An angry grumble arose from the crowd, whereat Smoky raised his voice and went on: "Under the European rules, that is. Under Rooshian rules, I may say, the house wins all bets when mousie quits. But we're playing American rules, and the house will furnish a new mousie free of charge. Now, how can we offer more than that?"

The quitter mouse was returned to the cage. A new mouse—smaller, obviously female, but just as lively as the first—was put into the glass box. Honker clutched Beansie by the arm.

"Come on outside," he whispered. "I think I'm going to swoon if this keeps up."

They managed to fight their way to the door of the tent just as the lightning flashed behind them. Somebody whooped, "A thousand dollars! Dog my cats if I didn't win a thousand dollars on number nine. Put that mousie back in, Mr. Croupier, and let's see her try again!"

"Did you hear that?" Beansie said. "He just lost a thousand-dollar bet for us, dern the dern luck!"

They faced each other. Honker's amber eyes were rolling wildly, and he had to struggle for his voice. "You better pray ol' Smoky loses a few more thousand-dollar bets for us in a hurry, boy!" he choked. "That's the richest game I ever see in my life. Why, we're at least ten thousand dollars winner right now."

"Oh! I see what you mean. If we win too much, they'll get sore and won't play any more."

"Something like that."

"I did notice that the mouse hardly ever hits a hole where there's a lot of money down. That sure is lucky for us."

"Something like that."

Another roar of excitement from someone in the tent as another high roller cashed in on a big bet. "Let's you and me go over and set down somewhere, Beansie," said Honker. "I ain't as young as I used to be, and my heart won't stand this strain."

"Look, Mr. Cahoon, there's Perfessor Blythe, the man that sold you the shovel."

Blythe spotted them almost at the same moment. He leaned sharply to the right, ready to take off in a sprint, but he leaned too far for the condition he was in and fell flat on his face. Honker went over and helped him up.

"Better watch that, Perfessor, you old fool. You might hurt yourself," he said.

"You—you ain't going to lynch me, Honker?" Blythe quavered.

Honker shook his head. "No. You tricked me, but you did live up to your guarantee."

"Are you sick, Honker, or just out of your mind?"

"Don't tempt me now. You behold before you a man unsteady of spirit, but don't push your luck."

The Perfessor faced him bravely, squinting at him with drunken gravity through his glasses. "You're not the Honker Cahoon I used to know," he said at last. "First, you run Dewey Score out of town like a yellow cur-dog, and now you don't even mind being cheated by me."

"You cheated me legal, like I said."

"Yes, but if you turned me upside down, you could still shake five or six dollars out of me. What's going on here? Listen, Honker, what's going on in that tent you put up?"

"I ain't got the heart to tell you. Go on in and find out for yourself," said Honker.

"That's exactly what I'll do! Something is rotten in Denmark, as the bard said, when you stand there like an innocent babe and let me keep my ill-gotten gains. Curse it, Honker—you take all the pleasure out of cheating you, when you don't resent it."

They watched him reel to the tent and push his way inside. Men made way for him, as they always did for the Perfessor. Honker started across the street.

"Shouldn't we wait and help Mr. O'Neill in case he needs us?" Beansie worried.

"He won't need the likes of you and me, Beansie—not with that brain of his'n! I'm just a penny-ante scoundrel, like the Perfessor. Smoky belongs up there with Gould and Jim Hill and the schoolbook trust. I need to set down and rest my feet and my brains."

They sat down under a tree and listened to the din from inside the tent. Smoky had learned quickly how to handle his crowd. The bets were coming down faster now, and the "romps" of the galvanized mousies occurred more frequently. Men went broke in the tent and came out, glassy-eyed but not discouraged, to go back to their jobs or their claims for more money.

A winner came out now and then, jingling $1,000, $2,500—one with $4,000. Most of the new trade seemed to come from the Silverado. Several of the winners immediately crossed the street and went into the Silverado, to display their winnings.

It was no surprise to either Honker or Beansie when Bill Shenker came out of the Silverado and started across the street too. He saw them sitting under the tree and stopped to call out to Honker.

"Hey there, Honker! Don't you forget that I've got three dressed beeves coming to me tonight."

"I ain't forgot. They'll be ready for you," Honker replied dispiritedly.

Bill got as far as the door of the tent, where he stood on tiptoe to watch what was going on inside. They saw him flinch back from the glare and racket as someone pulled the rope to start a mousie on a new romp. They could hear Smoky without making out his words and knew by the tone and tempo when he began urging the miners to put down their bets for another romp.

"Time to have a little talk with Bill, I reckon," Honker

said, "and this time, I can look forward to it with a full heart and a clean conscience. Come on, kid."

Bill turned on his heel to face them. "You—you're responsible for this, Honker!" he said thickly. "You and this low-down Smoky O'Neill is partners."

"That's right, Bill."

"Well, I ain't going to stand for it. That's a crooked game of some kind."

"Now, all you got to do is prove that—and even if you could, who would listen to you? Bill, you said it in front of witnesses: You wouldn't touch roulette no way in the world! You said anybody could have roulette that wanted it."

"I meant wheel roulette. Whoever heard of electric mouse roulette anyway?"

"I did."

"Well, it's crooked, I bet you double to one."

Honker extended his arm and pointed a trembling forefinger at the tent. "Go in there and you can get five to one. It pays five to one *every time!* How often do you pay five to one on your craps tables? You just go ahead in there, with your tightwad reputation, and try to tell anybody that it's a crooked game. I dare you!"

"I won't stand for it! Look—here comes the Perfessor. Poor old soak, I bet they even cleaned him out. Come here, Perfessor. I want to talk to you."

"Can't. Haven't got time," Blythe replied.

"What have you got to do that's so important?"

"Got to spend some of my winnings, my beautiful winnings, on your dirty, rotten, cheap, overpriced whisky."

"Your *winnings?*" Bill shouted.

Blythe brandished a fistful of gold coin and paper currency at him. "I left after playing three games. Started with six dollars, and I've got seven hundred and fifty here. Come on, Bill—I'll buy drinks for the house if you'll wait on us personally, with your own dainty hands."

Bill walked dazedly after him. They vanished into the Silverado.

"Boy, the Perfessor sure must be lucky," said Beansie.

"Something like that," said Honker. "Come on, we better go inside and help Smoky shut down the game. One thing sure, we've got to run it just two or three or four hours a day, and that's something neither one of us ever thought of."

"How come, Mr. Cahoon?"

"Got to give the fellas time to go out and earn more money, kid. Even a sheep gets time to grow more wool."

They sat in the cabin in the clearing, counting money, until long after dark.

The net income for the day was $18,840.

"Sure, and you're right about giving them time to grow more fleece, Honker," said Smoky. "Tell you what, after this, we'll open only for three hours each evenin' and stay closed up by day."

"Good idee," said Honker.

"Excuse me," said Beansie, "but I'd favor shutting down at night and running by day. It's too easy if somebody's going to stick you up, at night."

"The bye is right as rain! Verra well then, we'll open again on the morrow at the same time, run two or three hours, and shut down. Ah, wid two such partners as I've got now, to think of the things I've forgot, how can we not become millionaires before snowfall?"

Honker cleared his throat. "Another thing: it might be better to start figuring *four* partners."

Smoky studied him. "Blythe, you mean?"

"Yes."

"Yis. He caught on fast. Always betted the number wid the least on it. The crowd loved to see him win. Don't yez think he'll be satisfied wid that?"

Smoky's Irish brogue seemed to have returned in all its richness. He's Irish when he's happy and feeling good, Beansie decided, British when it pays and plain old American the rest of the time. . . .

"Mebbe for a few days," said Honker. "But my guess is a partnership. It ain't human nature to settle for less."

Smoky laughed joyously. "Who cares? Sure, and there's enough for all of us, lads."

CHAPTER TWELVE

The Perfessor, Judson Blythe, walked faster and faster as he neared the bar in the Silverado. It was almost deserted, thanks to the action across the street, where the game of mouse roulette still went on. Blythe rapped sharply on the bar with his knuckles.

"Set out your best, my good man—the whole bottle! Step lively, varlet. I am about to assuage the strongest appetite known to man—the thirst of a drunk who has money in his pocket," he said.

"First," said the bartender, "let's see the money."

With a hand that shook violently, Blythe dribbled the stack of gold pieces out on the bar. "There you are. Coin of the realm, my good man."

The barkeep sorted it swiftly with his fingertips. "Seven hundred and fifty. Well say, Perfessor, you kin stay drunk as a hog on that for a whole month."

"Drunk as a *what?*"

"You heard me. A hog."

"I, sir, am not a hog. A drunk, yes—I own up to that cheerfully, sir. But don't call me a hog."

"Oh, shoot, Perfessor—you're like any other drunk," the bartender said, twisting the cork to break the seal of a quart bottle of the finest bonded whisky. "You may be educated, you may even be entertaining at times. But the best I can say for you, Perfessor, is that you're an educated, entertaining hog."

Blythe reached for the bottle but did not quite touch it. His hand came back, shaking so hard he had to grip it with the other. He stared at himself in the mirror behind the bar.

"To be sure, to be sure," he muttered. "I never noticed it before, but you're right—I am a hog! And a man is better off dead than surviving as a hog."

"Oh, don't take it so hard! Drink your drink, Perfessor. You ain't no worse than any other hog."

Blythe scrambled his money together and dropped it carelessly into his pocket. "No sir. Now that I have met my swinish soul, face to face—never again! I'll probably die from it, but I have just quit drinking."

The bartender laughed. "Oh, sure—for about thirty minutes at the outside. Sorry if I hurt your feelings, Perfessor. Go on, drink your whisky."

But Blythe tottered outside and leaned against Bill Shenker's bull wagon. He looked at the miners who were passing in and out of the tent across the street, as though meeting them for the first time.

"And I have been looking down on them. A few of them may possibly be lower than I am—possibly. But there are hopes for me, because I have money in my pocket. If I can just stay sober until they open the mouse game again tomorrow, I'll have more. Now, how can I stay sober? There I have a real problem."

He knew he could not think clearly so close to Bill Shenker's bar. He staggered off down the street, his eyes on the ground, his overstrained mind struggling with his problem.

In the office shanty of the big mine over at Stairsteps, two men sat talking in low voices. The door was securely locked, but they had some old-timers on their crew, men who had worked coal mines or hard-rock mines all their lives. It would not be strange if a few had become suspicious of locked doors.

"If we pay the crew," said one, "how much will we have left?"

"One dollar and forty-four cents," said the other.

"And if we don't pay them?"

"Figure it for yourself. Thirteen hundred and seventy-seven men at two dollars a day for seven days. Multiply, and then add a dollar forty-four. I make it nineteen thousand two hundred and seventy-nine dollars and forty-four cents, and since that's the exact amount in the strongbox, I think we can assume that the books balance, Jimmy."

Jimmy clenched his fists and looked across the desk with burning eyes. "Maynard, I know we've been in lean rock lately, but the silver's there. It's *got* to be there! We've got our hands on a fortune if we can only hold out a little longer."

Maynard, who was the older and larger of the two, smiled genially. "We've been talking that way all summer, Jimmy. We owe fifteen thousand in bills in San Francisco and Sacramento, and we've got a credit balance of about eighteen dollars in the silver office there."

"But what can we do?"

"I don't know about *you*, but I'm selling you my share of the mine for—let's see, what's half of what we have left? I make it ninety-six hundred and thirty-nine dollars and seventy-two cents. Shortly after dark I'll be on my way down the mountain. I have the fastest horse in camp. Yours is next fastest. My suggestion is that you be about six feet behind me."

"And abandon the mine? Lose everything?"

Maynard smiled. "We have already lost everything. I put up the money, my lad. I've dribbled a hundred thousand down your hard-rock rat hole. Well, I took your judgment, and I don't bear you any ill will. But all things come to an end, and our mine is over—finished, done for, kaput!"

"But you're a rich man, Maynard. You can keep us going until we hit the lode. Your father was—"

"A millionaire several times over, yes he was. He left it all to me, but he left me a bit of advice that has been worth more than all his money to me. 'Son,' he said to me once, 'there are three things that no man can afford to support no matter how rich he is. They are a horse that always comes in second, a woman who always comes in first, and a mine that never comes in at all.'"

"When you figger on pulling out?"

"As soon as it's dark enough. Coming with me?"

"What else can I do? If you take half the payroll and leave me only enough to pay off half the men . . ."

About an hour before sunset two men forded the Mokelumne and spurred their horses into a trot up the wagon road that led—they had been told—to Camp Corinth. They rode good horses, both with the Bar Anchor brand, but the men were shabbily dressed and gaunt with hunger. The beefy one in the lead looked back over his shoulder.

"I still don't like the idee of riding into no mining camp after dark, Merle," he said. "What if we run into that old yaller-eyed gunnie from Texas first off? *He* knows these ain't our horses. You'll have your pick then, getting hung for a horse thief or shooting it out with him."

"Lou, you can scare yourself to death thinking when you're hungry," said the bony, chinless youth with bad teeth, who rode in the rear. "He don't scare me none. All I ask with him is an even draw."

"Yes, but what if you don't get it?"

"Then it'll be your fault. We ain't facing him man to man—can't you get that through your thick head? It's two of us against him."

"I still don't like it. I never heard of Honker Cahoon, and anything I don't know about, it bothers me."

"It don't bother me! Neither did Dewey Score, you remember. *He* was the one that told us all about the famous Honker Cahoon."

"Yes, but you know and I know, the way he described Honker Cahoon, it's the same man we tried to stick up down there on the Nevada trail."

"He maybe bluffed Dewey Score out of camp," Merle Watson said with a nervous giggle, "but he don't scare me none. I want to see if he's as fast as he thinks he is."

"You'll get yourself killed thataway, Merle."

"And maybe I won't. My daddy, he used to brag I was the fastest man in the whole world with a hand gun. And I bet I am."

"After dark?"

"It's just as dark for him as it is for me. And I told you—we'll get him between us, and this time he ain't going to talk us out of it."

I sure hope you're right, Lou Burnside thought, because I don't trust your daddy's judgment one bit, and I don't trust yours neither. The way he looked at us out of them yella eyes—he fairly gives me a chill, just to remember it.

Smoky O'Neill had planned mouse roulette for so many years, had gone over its details in his mind so often, he had come prepared for everything. When they closed down the game for the night, he removed only one handful of wires from it. He attached instead an alarm bell that would be triggered by anyone pushing against the wires stretched around the interior of the tent.

They left the flap of the tent open and two big lanterns burning brightly inside. Returning to the cabin in the clearing, they took with them only the maze of wires that Smoky had removed, and the cage of mice. The four mice that had "worked" in the game that day, Smoky freed just outside the cabin.

"Go on, enjoy yourselves, mousies!" he said with an affectionate chuckle. "Spread the word about that it's not bad a-tall, a-tall. Ah, little mousies, ye'll be famous among all your kindred from now on."

They went into the cabin. "What are you going to do with all the money?" Beansie asked. "I sure would hate to get stuck up for it now that we've got it."

"They may steal it from us," Smoky said, "but it will be some time before they can enjoy it. Watch!"

He took out the strongbox he had built over the years, adding to it as he had time and money. It weighed nearly a hundred pounds empty. It was made of quarter-inch armor-plate steel, with a lid held on by six tool-steel bolts. Each bolt was locked by an enormous padlock.

"Six keys it takes to open it," Smoky said. "Two for each of us. It'll take a blacksmith to open it, and he'll want two days at least. We can let it set here in plain sight with no worry. Or we can bury it, as yez like."

"I've got a better idee," said Honker. "Let the Washos take care of it for us. Nobody will suspect them, and even if they did, they've got to find the Washos and then somehow talk them into handing over the box."

"First rate! Here's two keys for you, Honker, and two for Beansie. Now we'll lock up the money. You go find your Indians, Honker, and Beansie and I will wait here with the money."

Honker had no sooner left for the Washo village than Bill Shenker arrived in his bull wagon for the meat. He refused to leave until Honker got back. Bill had passed the stage of indignant anger. Now he was hurt that his oldest and best friend should go into competition across the street from his Silverado.

"I did *not* go into competition with you, blame it all!" Honker honked. "You *said* you wouldn't have a roulette game in the house. You said *anybody* could have roulette that wanted it."

"I said a roulette *wheel!* You ain't playing no roulette there. That is a fraud on the public, and you only make it more dishonest by calling it roulette."

"In what way is it a frog? Them's mice!"

"I said *fraud*, you old fool! Whoever heard of betting on mice?"

"Half of Camp Corinth. You seen them your own self."

Bill had been leaning against his near ox. He straightened up, shaking his head sorrowfully. "I hope I don't have to take steps against you, Honker. I know it's an offense against public decency to book bets on a daggone mouse, so it stands to reason it's against the law too."

147

"Bill, you come around here and lie about us, and talk about frogs and so forth, and try to deny the hard-working miners of Camp Corinth their own innocent fun. You've got me so worked up, I don't see how I can go on furnishing fresh beef for you. In fact, we quit!"

"You can't do that! You already caused me enough trouble. Listen! How about we make a deal, Honker? How about I trade you a one-fourth interest in the Silverado for a half interest in mouse roulette?"

"I thought you said it was against decency and breaking the law besides."

"Don't goad me, Honker! I'll deal—a fourth of the Silverado for half of your game."

"No! Do you think we're loco, or what?" An idea seemed to strike Honker suddenly. He squinted and tugged at his mustache. "How about a *third* of mouse roulette for *all* of the Zigzag T, livestock as well as land?"

"You must think I'm sap-headed as a cottonwood sucker."

"That's the only deal we'll take—a third of the game for all of your ranch."

Bill, still mumbling to himself, picked up his prod, grunted to his brindle team of oxen, and started his load back to town. "You won't listen to reason," he called back over his shoulder, "I'll run you out of camp, that's what I'll do. This is your last chance."

"Frogs!" Honker said scathingly. "Can't even tell a frog from a mouse."

The Indians lurked in the brush until Bill was out of sight. They exclaimed over the weight of Smoky's strongbox, but it did not dismay them. They lashed it to a long pole and headed cheerfully back to their village, two men on each end of the pole handling the weight easily.

When Honker looked around for Beansie, he was gone.

Beansie followed Bill's wagon on foot at first. He was not sure if he had seen a horseman lurking back in the timber between the cabin and Camp Corinth, but he knew that Bill did not allow anyone from the camp to trespass in the clearing. He had remained out of sight while Honker and Bill argued. The Washos themselves could have been no stealthier when he set out after the wagon.

It was almost dark. He stayed out of the winding road and slipped from tree to tree, carrying the .30-30 in his hand. He stayed a good one hundred yards behind the slow-moving wagon and the plodding, dejected Bill.

Less than a quarter of a mile from camp, a tall man was waiting beside his tied horse. It was a fine horse, restless from being tied. The man's face was shadowed by the wide brim of his expensive, flat-crowned hat.

"What kind of a hornswoggle is this?" he greeted Bill. "I didn't see no boy there!"

"He was there all right. I don't know how you could miss him. He's taller than either of them other two, about my height."

Beansie shivered.

"Well then, he'd be the wrong boy anyhow, but I don't know why I didn't see him."

"Come to think of it, he went into the cabin when old Honker started jawing at me."

"Honker—this is the old gunman you was telling me about? Seems I've heard his name someplace or other."

"I wouldn't be surprised. I hear he's one of the best."

The tall man snorted. "I'd know about him if he was. I got a good notion to go see for myself."

"I told you, I don't care for strangers hanging around my place there."

"And I told you I don't care what you care for. I want to get a look at that boy kid."

"I don't reckon Honker is going to take too dad-blamed kindly to you pestering around there."

"He can take his chances same as I do."

"I sure wish you wouldn't. Just let well enough alone. Honker is already on the prod."

"How you look at Honker and how I look at him is two different things."

The tall man untied his horse and stepped up into the saddle. He shifted his gun belt, took a good feel of the butt of the gun, and gave the horse a nudge with his heels.

Beansie sprinted as hard as he could back to the cabin. His horse and Honker's still had not been unsaddled. He untied his and led it deep into the timber. He stood there in the dark with his hand on the horse's nostrils while the tall stranger's fine horse passed on its way to the cabin.

Beansie mounted then and shook the reins over his startled horse's neck. The horse was going at a hard gallop, belly down and nose extended, when it passed Bill Shenker and his bull wagon. The startled Bill almost climbed up on the near ox's back when the pounding horse went by in the dark.

CHAPTER THIRTEEN

Smoky O'Neill was warming up a skilletful of beans, and Honker was on his knees beside the stove, prodding up the fire and grumbling because Beansie was not there to do it, when the knock came at the door.

Honker was on his feet in a movement like that of a striking snake. His Adam's apple jumped alarmingly, and his hand went to the butt of his gun. His jaw worked, but no sound came out.

"Just a minute, just a minute!" Smoky said as the knock was repeated. "Why don't yez kick the door in while you're at it, belike?"

He flung the door open and beheld a tall and extremely well-dressed man with the saddest expression either he or Honker had ever seen on a human being. More conspicuous than his sorrowing face, however, was the way he carried his hands—in plain sight, too high to be handy to his .45, and palms forward in a silent appeal for peace.

"Which one of you is Honker Cahoon?" he said.

"I am," Honker said. He was nervous enough to sound more belligerent than he felt.

"Wonder if I could talk to you a minute," said the caller. "My name is Smith, Quayle Smith. That's like the bird, only you spell it with a *y: Q, u, a, y, l, e.*"

Honker could only stare at him. "That strikes me as right interesting," he said, "if you take interest in that sort of thing, which I don't. What can we do for you?"

"I'm looking for a runaway boy, and I heard you had one living with you."

"We got a boy, all right, only I don't know where the varmint is, or if he's a runaway or not."

"Yella-brown hair, fourteen years old, about five feet five inches tall?"

"Don't seem to be the right boy, but you can wait and look him over. This one is about eighteen likely. He claims to be twenty-one, which I don't believe nohow, and he stands close to six feet."

"He ain't around nowhere?"

"He's supposed to be. I don't know where the varmint run off to."

"Where's he come from, do you know?"

"I never asked, because I didn't care. A boy gets to that age, his business is his'n."

"What name does he claim?"

"Johnny Smith," Honker said with a grin, "same as everybody I ever knowed that is giving the wrong handle for the first time. I call him Beansie, and he answers to it, and I don't know what you can expect more from a name."

The tall stranger's expression grew even more lugubrious. "Don't appear to be the right boy at all, but I sure would like to see him, just to make sure. Don't seem to me you're taking very good care of him if he can just waltz off like this whenever he likes."

"That don't seem to me to be none of your business if it comes to that. *I* didn't ask for custody of him; *he* wished himself onto *me*. And he's old enough to answer for his own sins."

The stranger sighed. "But it's mighty strange he dis-

appears just when I want to see him. I don't aim to be
critical of your way of doing things—"

"Then don't!"

"Now hold on there, Mr. Cahoon—I ain't used to being
talked to like that."

Without realizing it, Honker had slipped back into the
character of The Old Gunnie—sage, a little crotchety,
disillusioned with the world, more tolerant of people's
mistakes than in his hot-tempered youth, and yet not
ready to let people walk all over him.

"Well," he said, "I feel bad about that, yes I do, because I'm used to talking just any old how I feel like talking. So if your feelings is hurt, why, all I can say is that
it's too bad."

"Now hold on there, don't push me! In my younger
days, before I learned patience and self-control, I used
to never get my feelings *hurt*. But you could ruffle them
pretty easy at your peril."

"And in *my* younger days I used to go around looking
for people to ruffle their feelings. But I'm past all that
now, lucky for you."

"Lucky for me? I reckon you never heard of me, did
you?"

"I heard of them all, but I'd bet you never heard of me,
Honker Cahoon, either."

"In my wild young days, when I was mostly on the
wrong side of the law, I was knowed by the name of
Worried Smith. I wouldn't let *nobody* know I was called
by no such name as Quayle, and you can just guess how
I got to be called Worried. Well, you just ask anybody
that knowed me if it was safe to fool around ruffling the
feelings of Worried Smith—"

Honker went stone-deaf. It all came back to him, the

153

whole fanciful tale he had told Beansie of how he broke
Worried Smith of his train-robbing habit and made an
honest and self-respecting citizen of him against his will.
The kid would come long-legging in any minute and
know the minute he saw Worried Smith's worried expression who he was.

Honker's brain stopped working as his mouth took over
and The Old Gunnie arose once more in all his fictitious
fire as the youth he had never spent came back from nowhere. His voice took on that strident, shattering, over-
bearingly raucous tone that had given him his nickname:

"Oh, you make me plumb tired talking thataway. Like
I was telling this boy of mine, Beansie, you're all just a
bunch of troublemaking riffraff, and I'd be ashamed to
go around admitting I was the famous Worried Smith. I
knowed you the minute you came in here, you miserable
old troublemaking fourflusher, and if you think you can
come into Honker Cahoon's house and flourish around
with your danged riffraff bragging, why, just go for your
gun. That's all I've got to say, mister—if you *really* want
to look worried, just go for your gun! You're all just a
bunch of fourflushers, you and Lou Burnside and the
whole Watson tribe, and Dewey Score besides. Now
either keep a polite and civil tongue in your head, or get
out of this here cabin."

Smith raised his hands a little higher, still keeping them
palms forward. He said, "I've put all that behind me,
Cahoon, and I wish you would too. It's just ridiculous for
men our age to be talking gunplay like a couple of young
troublemaking bucks."

Honker still could not hear him. He had stopped for
breath, and now he had it back. "I wish an old retired
gunman like me could stay retired in peace, because there

ain't nothing sillier on earth than an old man trying to act like a young one, although I can if I have to. So either pull your weapon or back down, and that's my final word on this or any other subject to you tonight."

He still could not hear, but he could see, and he could lip-read a little. Worried Smith's face lighted up and looked less like the next of kin's at a funeral, and he came into the cabin with his hand outstretched. His lips were saying silently, "Shake! Let's shake hands on that."

They shook hands. Honker's hearing returned, and his entire body went cold as the evening breeze from the open door chilled the sweat that encased him.

"I ain't seen your runaway son, Smith," he growled, "but you can hang around until this little varmint gets here and satisfy yourself."

"No, I made enough of a nuisance of myself," said Smith. "For a minute, sir, I was tempted to go back to the old ways, when I seen the famous Honker Cahoon in front of me, and me with a gun on my flank. But like I say, it's just ridiculous for men our age to talk about shooting it out, so I'll just say thank you, sir, and good night."

They shook hands once more, and in a sudden eruption of good will, Honker walked outside with Smith to where his horse was tied to the corral fence.

"I never was misfavored with any family," said Honker, "and from all the trouble they seem to cause, I don't regret it a bit. This boy I got on my hands is worry enough. All he can talk about is famous gunmen! I try to tell him they're mostly just riffraff."

"And who would know better than you?" said Smith. "Not that it ain't the truth. When I look back at the way I put in my youthful years, going around holding up

155

trains and looking for fast-draw artists to face down, why, I just about despise myself."

"I can see how you would. I'm glad I'm retired."

"So am I. You saved me making a fool of myself tonight, Cahoon. You're prob'ly in pretty good practice yet with a gun."

"Well, yes, I reckon I am."

"I'm not. Listen, who all did you shoot it out with? I know I've heard the name Honker Cahoon, but I just don't recollect the other parties in the gun fights."

"I don't care to talk about it. They're just troublemaking riffraff is the way I look at it."

"I agree with you plumb to the line fence."

They shook hands, and Smith mounted his horse and galloped away. Honker went back into the cabin. Smoky O'Neill had the beans still warming on the stove.

"I wonder how long this Smith has been missing his kid," he said.

"He didn't mention. Why?" said Honker.

"Do you really figger Beansie to be eighteen?"

"No more than that. Why?"

"He ever say who his family was?"

"No, but they're cattlemen. He knows how to work cattle, and all he wants out of life is to own a cow outfit of his own. Why you asking this?"

"It's the fall of the year," Smoky said pensively, "and a cattleman can spare himself to be away from his place. From the looks of Beansie's clothes, he's been gone quite some time. Now, suppose—just suppose—he happens to be Worried Smith's son and he run away last summer sometime, or spring. A boy that age grows so fast, his own father wouldn't know him. And Beansie just don't seem to me to be as old as eighteen."

Honker said nothing. In a moment Smoky went on: "In me fourteenth year, I did all of me last growing. I was too big for me clothes and too big for me place in me father's house. 'Twasn't much I grew after I left there, because, for one thing, I went on short rations, like a boy will when he's so smart about earning his own way in the world. But I had to go, Honker! I was eating me daddy out of house and home, and I couldn't stand taking his orders, and when he next heard from me, half the world was come between us. 'Twas how I came to America. Not exactly a runaway boy, you see, because I'd done a man's work for many's the month."

"When I was fourteen," said Honker, "I was an old man. Well, well! This cub has sure enough done some growing since his daddy last laid eyes on him."

They heard Beansie grumbling at his horse outside as he stripped off the saddle and bridle, haltered it, and gave it hay for the evening. Honker and Smoky exchanged smiles as the youth came through the door.

"I'm late," said Beansie.

"Do tell!" said Honker. "There was a man here to see you, I think."

"Not to see me," Beansie said, avoiding Honker's eyes.

"We didn't give you away."

"There's nothing to give away."

Honker shrugged. "Have it your own way. We don't want to pry into your business, Quayle, but—"

"*What?*" The kid had been about to hang his hat in the corner. He flung it across the room instead and came at Honker with his fists up. "Don't you call me that! Don't you dare! Nor Junior either!"

"All right, but you've give yourself away, you know,

157

and put me and Smoky up a tree. We lied to your dad, even if we didn't know we was doing it."

"You didn't tell on me, did you?"

"No, but—"

"Please don't, not until I'm rich."

Honker frowned at him, puzzled. "Whoever heard of a kid being rich when he's only fourteen years old?"

"Please, Mr. Cahoon! You've got to promise. You don't know what it's like to be the oldest son of a famous man."

"I never knowed what it was like to be the son of anybody. Well, well—this is going to take some thinking over. But all right, we'll keep your secret a while yet."

The two men held their horses down to a quiet walk as they neared the wagon road in the dark. The big man, Maynard, rode in the lead, puffing rhythmically on a fat cigar.

"Should hit it soon, Jimmy," he said over his shoulder. "We'll make better time then. The more miles between us and Camp Corinth, the better I'll feel."

"I thought you said you was going to divide up what money was left," said Jimmy.

"The moment we can spare the time, Jimmy."

"You sure hang on to it as long as you can!"

Maynard untied the small valise that hung from his saddle horn. "Then you hang onto it yourself."

"No, I didn't mean that, Maynard. You can—"

"*Take it!* We're partners. You did your fool's best to bring in a paying mine. I was a fool to believe you could do it, but I'm still your partner, and I live up to my deals. You carry the money."

Jimmy took the valise. They came out of the brush on

the wagon road and let their horses take the easy down-
ward grade to the Mokelumne. They had ridden no more
than a quarter of a mile when a snarling voice out of the
darkness made them both haul their horses back on their
haunches.

"Reach for the sky! You with the cigar—get that other
hand up there where we can see it! You with the satchel—
walk your horse on down, nice and slow, and let's take a
look at what's in it."

"Nothing but a few handkerchiefs and my shaving
things," Maynard said easily. "How did you spot us, may
I ask? The light of my cigar?"

A shriller voice, with a hint of giggle in it, came from
the dark brush beside the road. "See if he's got any more
of them cigars on him too. Man as careless as him, smoking in the dark, just ain't to be trusted with good cigars."

Maynard and Jimmy got a good look at only the big,
obese man in the center of the road. The smaller,
slighter man remained a dim shadow to them. The two
robbers did not bother to open the satchel. They relieved
their victims of their wallets, Maynard also yielding up
a fine gold watch.

"They ain't armed. I'm going to let them go," the big
one said.

"Just get their cigars too," said the giggling shadow
in the brush.

Maynard handed over two cigars from his waistcoat
pocket. "All I've got, and they were to have lasted me
until I got to Sacramento. For your friend, with my com-
pliments."

The fat one took the cigars. "Just head on down the
road, and stay alive," he said.

"That is my only interest. Good night to you."

159

Maynard half expected a shot in the back as he rode down the slope, but it did not come. Jimmy seemed to be close to tears when he caught up with him.

"How much have you got left, Jimmy?" said Maynard.

"Pocket change. Less than a dollar."

"About the same with me."

"I thought you had a gun."

"I do, in my saddlebag. It's only a ticket on the underground railway once they get the drop on you."

"Give it to me. I'll go back and shoot those fellows in the back."

"You could try, surely. But even if you succeeded, we're still close to Camp Corinth. How would you explain being out on the road the night before payday, if someone rode out to investigate? No, Jimmy my boy, the faster we can get down this mountain, the better off we'll be."

CHAPTER FOURTEEN

Camp Corinth awakened to a white world of heavy fog. At the hard-rock mine the blast of a whistle stirred out late-sleeping men whose first cheerful thought was that this was payday. The office shanty was closed, but they were used to this. No one noticed that two horses—the strongest, fastest, and best—were missing from the corral behind the comfortable tent where the bosses lived.

Bill Shenker awakened as slowly as possible. He dreaded the day, because he would take in several thousand dollars less than usual—perhaps many, many thousands of dollars less than usual. And he did not know what to do about it.

All up and down Fat Tree Creek, men were out to their placer works as soon as it was light enough to see. Other men, gophering back into the canyon wall by ones and twos and threes, searching for gold and silver and, often enough, finding at least traces of it, were also early to work. Most had slept a light sleep that was filled with visions of mice scampering into the right hole. These were flat broke; yet with the witless optimism of prospectors, there was not a man among them who was not sure that this was *his* day. Either he would strike it rich in the sands of the creek or the mountainside, or today mousie would go straight to the right hole.

In the little cabin in the clearing, Beansie, whose real

name was Quayle Smith, Junior, was the first to awaken. He had given up his bunk to Smoky O'Neill and was sleeping on the floor, near the stove. Mice scampering across his bed aroused him, but this time he did not hurl imprecations and deadly objects at them. He merely turned over on his stomach and watched them scamper.

Go, you little rascals! he thought. I'm going to leave something good out for you to eat every night after this. 'Tain't fair, you do all the work and we make all the money. . . .

Lou Burnside and Merle Watson had to dismount and walk when the fog closed in. There had been enough moonlight for them to find their way on the wagon road earlier, but now they were like blind men, leading their horses and feeling their way. When daylight finally did seep in, it was hard to see a massive tree trunk twenty feet away.

"Let's see what's in the valise, Lou," Watson said as soon as there was enough light.

"What's the hurry?" Burnside said sullenly.

"The way that one fella tightened up when t'other'n handed it over, I got a hunch we hit it rich."

"We'll shorely find out. Let's look."

Burnside untied the valise and opened it. "Just what he said. Couple of good razors. Hone. Strop. Brush and mug and soap. And some handkerchiefs."

Watson pawed through the valise, letting the things fall to the ground. He threw the valise down after them. "Lou, something's wrong here. I got a notion to go after them two again."

"Why?"

"We missed something. I can feel it."

162

"You go if you want," said Burnside, "but I'm going to try my luck in Camp Corinth. You *feel* there was money on them two pilgrims. But I *know* there's money in a big mining camp."

Watson reluctantly plodded after him. They were able to mount and ride into Camp Corinth a couple of hours later, when the sun had risen higher. It was an eerie kind of sunlight, in which the dark tents of the camp were still hidden from the riders until they got within a hundred yards. They walked their tired, hungry horses down the middle of the street, sizing things up with the wildcat wariness of fugitives.

The odor of fresh coffee, of stew warming up on a big stove, made their eyes as well as their mouths water. "How much money you got left, Merle?" Lou asked in a low voice. "I declare, I'm so dratted hungry, I ain't going to be worth burying if I don't eat soon."

"Almost a dollar." Watson giggled. "Hell of a pair of highwaymen we are! I'm so weak I don't think I could lift my gun if I knowed there was a thousand dollars to be had."

"A dollar will buy us breakfast. Let's eat and then find some place where we can catch some sleep and graze and rest the horses. Then we can look this place over and find out who's got the money. We'll be fresh, and so will our horses, when it's time to run for it."

"Makes sense."

They followed their noses to the heartbreaking sign ALL MEALS $3.00. They could only stare at each other with grief-filled eyes. No doubt they could obtain breakfast at gun point, but only by giving up any plan of making a stake by the same means later in the day.

"Lou," Watson whimpered, "we got to eat, we just *got* to. But how?"

Burnside's dull slab of a face hardened. His small eyes narrowed. "I reckon," he said, "I'll have to sacrifice my own daddy's gold watch, that I've packed all these years."

"A gold watch? I never knowed you had a gold watch!"

Burnside dismounted and reached into a saddlebag. "All these years I've packed it and never parted with it. I reckon this is the end of the trail though."

"Let me see that watch."

Burnside handed it over. "Ain't she a beauty?"

Watson studied the watch, then slid out of the saddle with it still in his hand. His voice dropped almost to a whisper. "She sure is, and this ain't your daddy's watch either. This belongs to the same feller we took the money from, you dirty doublecrosser! You high-graded me, Lou! We split the money, and you kept this watch!"

"No such thing."

"You lie! You was the one searched him while I held the gun on him. That's a mistake I'll never make again with you, Lou."

"I swear it's my poor dead daddy's watch."

"Then how come it's got the initials V. K. R. on it?"

"I always wondered that myself," Burnside said with an expression of such childlike candor that it took the younger, smaller man's breath away. "Just be glad I saved it till now, Merle. We can eat on it."

"All right, but I make the deal—not you."

They tied their horses and went into the Silverado tent, where a dozen men were wolfing three-dollar plates of warmed-over beef stew at a slab counter made from a split log. Merle offered the watch in return for two breakfasts and twenty dollars in cash. The bearded man behind the counter laughed at them.

"I got a gunny-sack full of watches," he snorted.

"Not as good as this'n. Look it over."

The restaurant manager examined the watch carefully by candlelight. "Not bad. Tell you what I'll do. I'll feed you both, all you can eat, for this watch and your gun, cowboy."

They bargained. Watson knew covetousness when he saw it. The man wanted the watch. Watson held out until he got their breakfasts and two five-dollar gold pieces for the watch.

They ate copiously, mounted again, and went for a short ride around the camp. The din from the machinery at the hard-rock mine drew them like a magnet. When they saw the size of the operation, they looked at each other significantly. They both shook their heads however. There would be big money at a place like this, but it would take an army to steal it, and they did not even know where it was kept. And the office was not even open yet.

No, their best bet was a lively business on the street, after the sun came out and they could see well enough to make a judgment. They rode their horses across the creek and found a place where the animals could graze. They hobbled them and stretched out on the damp grass, and with their bellies full for the first time in days, they were quickly asleep.

Burnside awakened first. As best he could judge, it was well past noon. The fog was gone, and the sun was out. It was warmer than it had been this morning, but there was a clammy feeling in the air that warned him that winter was not far away in this elevation.

He stirred his partner with his toe. "Up on your feet, Merle! We got to hit somebody quick and be off for the coast this afternoon."

Watson came awake like a puma. "All right," he said as he beat his hat into shape over his leg, "but this time *you* hold the gun on them and *I'll* collect."

"You shore are a suspicious little runt!"

"Yes, us Watsons are all like that."

They caught their horses and removed their hobbles. The first person they saw when they rode into Camp Corinth was a white-haired man, afoot, helping himself along with a cane cut from a second-growth cottonwood sapling. A pair of glasses perched precariously on his aristocratic nose, and when he stopped in response to their hail, his hand began shaking violently.

"Wonder if you could tell me where to find Jim Robinson, the banker?" Burnside accosted him.

"No banker by that name here. The Wells Fargo is down the street yonder."

The white-haired man tottered off. There was no Jim Robinson of course, but it was more tactful to inquire about banks in this fashion. If there was only a Wells Fargo here, robbing a bank was out. Wells Fargo did not like to be robbed, and it had the far-flung facilities which made it possible to track down anyone foolish enough to try it and lucky enough to get away with it.

No, it would have to be some business house that kept cash on hand. They grinned contemptuously at each other as the Perfessor, Judson Blythe, hurried on up the street. Just some drunk shaking for his morning pickup, they thought. They would have been sorely chagrined to know that Blythe had been on the wagon for sixteen hours now and had $750 in cash on his ragged person.

They walked their horses on up the street. The Silverado was the biggest tent in camp, but all the action seemed to be centered in the tent across the street, which seemed to be just opening for business.

"Mouse roulette? What the devil is mouse roulette?" said Watson.

"I don't know," said Burnside, "but it sure seems to be getting the heavy play in this here town. Look, there goes that old drunk into the tent."

From inside the tent came a crisp and merry voice in a rich Irish brogue: "Wan minute more, gents, if yez please! Give me time to get me game ready, and we'll all have our sport together. Stand back, stand back, I beg yez!"

Burnside turned his horse so abruptly that it bumped violently into Watson's. "Out of sight!" he hissed out of the corner of his mouth. "There's Worried Smith. Slide off behind this tent here. Now what's he doing here anyway?"

"I don't know as I care," Watson said. "I heard so much about him, and I always wondered if he's as good with a gun as they say. How much you want to bet I'm faster?"

Burnside said harshly, "You tarnation fool, what have we got to bet? We've got to make a winter's stake here, you plumb imbecile, and get down to the coast where it's warm. You ain't starting no fancy gun fights now!"

"All right," Watson sighed, "but I bet he's long past his prime. I bet I'm faster than he is."

"There's your dad, Beansie," said Honker. "Now let's cut out this— Now where the dickens did he go?"

There was not even a ripple in the crowd in the tent to show which way the boy had gone. Honker tried to catch Smith's attention, but the former gunman was staring out the door of the tent toward the Silverado. There was no time to catch up with him, as he saw Worried Smith leave the tent, because Smoky O'Neill had dropped the first mouse into the glass cage. A roar went up from the eager crowd.

"Place your bets, gentlemen," Smoky intoned. "The mousie is about to make his run midst the crackle of lightning. Which hole will he choose, gents? Ah, but isn't he a foine one though! A big, strong boar-mouse, this one, ready to make someone a lot of money. Get your bets down, gentlemen. Bet your judgment and watch mousie scamper!"

The money came down swiftly—not so much as had fallen yesterday, because the crowd had been picked clean, and it would take weeks to replenish it to yesterday's affluence. Those who could not reach the table handed their money across for others to put down for them and called their bets aloud:

"Twenty dollars on five."

"Bet my ten on six for me, sport."

"Here, take my ten and put it on ten. Can't beat that for a combination—ten on ten."

"Put it on two for me, please, like a good fella."

"Nine for me. The ninth is my birthday."

The Perfessor had managed to reach the table. His eyes were wild, his complexion gray as ashes. His mouth worked, and his chin trembled continuously. But his eye appeared sharp and his nerve steady. He held his money in his hand, waiting, it seemed, for some last-minute revelation on how to bet.

"Are we through? All through betting, gents? Then give the cord a yank, and let's watch mousie scamper!" said Smoky.

He swung the end of the rope out over the crowd. A hand grasped it and pulled. An excited sigh, like a wind rising suddenly in the pine tops, went through the crowd as the white lightning lighted the room. The mouse streaked across the cage and back. The clackers clacked, the buzzers buzzed.

The mouse found his hole, most of the crowd groaned, a few whooped with delight, and Honker saw Blythe snatch up a small heap of coins and slip them into his pocket. Smoky raked up the money of the losers and stacked it near his hands, which rested on the edge of the table. He stooped, recaptured the mouse, dropped him into the cage again, and brought out a fresh mouse.

"Another vigorous young male, gents, ready to scamper and make you some money. Bet your judgment and let's watch him scamper. Put your money on the mousie and take home five to one!"

Four times Honker saw the lightning flash and saw Smoky gather up the house's portion afterward. Four times, too, he watched the Perfessor chunk his five- or ten-dollar bet down at the last minute—and rake in his five-to-one winnings afterward. He knows more about this game than I do, for sure, Honker thought, with a grin. Best offhand judge of mouse flesh in the world, beyond a doubt. . . .

The pile of cash in front of Smoky amounted to around two thousand dollars by then, Honker estimated. He saw Smoky reach under the table to recapture the mouse that had made the last run. He saw him pause, the mouse still in his hand, to cock his ear and listen.

Their eyes met, and Smoky's gave Honker some kind of signal that Honker did not catch. Smoky turned and dropped the mouse into the cage with the other mice instead of putting it in the glass box. He used both hands to snatch up the money in front of him and the wires he always detached from the battery circuits.

"Closing down for a few minutes, gents. Let's cross to the Silverado, and the drinks are on us," he called out

169

sharply. "Everybody to the Silverado for free drinks on mousie."

He was gone before the crowd had time to do more than mutter. He came out of the crowd under Honker's very arm. "Come on, Honker—quick about it! Over to the Silverado," he hissed.

He towed Honker along by his arm. "I don't get it, Smoky. What's wrong?" Honker demanded.

The crowd trooped after them. Bill Shenker, all alone behind his almost-deserted bar, glared at them with red-rimmed, tragic eyes. Smoky dribbled a rain of five-dollar gold pieces on the bar.

"Drinks for everybody, sir. And if you'll take my advice, you'll just set out the bottles and run for it, like us," he said. "Come on, Honker!"

"Where to?"

"Is there a back way out of this place? Horses, man— find our horses!"

They were already out the back way, and Smoky was still running.

"What the dickens ails you, Smoky?" Honker demanded.

"There's one sound that ye never forget if ye've heard it once," said Smoky. "That's the roar of a mob. I swear I could hear one ten miles off—and this one is not that far away by any means. Run, man, run!"

Honker heard it then. In fact, he could already see them streaming across the flats from Stairsteps. They looked like an army to him. They had stopped howling, saving their breath for the work of destruction that lay ahead, but they had not slowed down.

The crew at the hard-rock mine had discovered that the management had decamped with the day's payroll.

CHAPTER FIFTEEN

Far into the night the mob raged. Honker, Beansie, and Smoky took turns riding through the timber to check up on it, although they could see the glare from the burning tents as far as the cabin in the clearing. By midnight the last fire had gone out. The moon shone pallidly on a few smoking ruins. Out of one rose a tall, squarish silhouette—Bill Shenker's enormous steel safe. The mob had pounded against it in vain. Even dynamite had failed to open it, because the departed mine management had not enough dynamite in stock to do the job.

"They're most of them asleep now," Honker reported when he came back a little after two in the morning. "They cleaned out Bill's drinkable stock before they set fire to the Silverado. I heard somebody say they drunk up three hundred cases."

"By morning we'll be able to slip through them, one hopes," Smoky said. "Ah, me poor mousie game, to be destroyed by the vileness of man before it had more than tried its wee little wings."

"That's the funny thing, Smoky. They didn't touch our tent. I thought first it was because it's back kind of next to the trees, but I talked to one fella. He said they was ready to lynch everybody but us," said Honker.

Smoky leaped to his feet. "They did? Then me precious electrical gear is safe?"

"Yes. They even fed the mice in the cage."

"Honker, do ye see now how it pays to maintain a state of virtue?" Smoky cried joyously. "All we have to do is pack it up and slip out like, before they change their minds."

"That'll take some doing," Honker said. "I think I'd sooner try to take raw meat away from a tiger. They can't wait to play mousie roulette again."

"But we must! We've got to get me game away from them."

"One thing we might try," Beansie said. "They'll all be hungry come morning. If we could get there with a few sides of fresh beef maybe they'd let us go."

"Pay off the mob that ruined him with Bill Shenker's beef?" said Honker, scandalized. "Boy, what kind of morals is that?"

"We won't steal it. We'll pay him for every pound of it," said Smoky. He added hastily, "Wholesale, of course. Can yez get yer Indians out now? So we can bring the beef there by daylight? Say ye can, Honker—please!"

"I can sure try."

There were nine steers left in the lot. By morning the carcasses of five were swinging from the trees. The other four, freshly dressed, were stacked in Smoky's wagon. The fog was as dense as it had been the night before. They worked hard and fast, hoping the fog would hold until they could get to the ashes of the camp, load up Smoky's equipment and be on their way before it cleared up.

Honker took the reins of Smoky's four broncs. They came furtively into camp just as the sun began to filter through the fog. A few restless souls were up and about, but most lay where they had fallen. It was a scene of desolation that Honker would never forget—several hundred burned tents and close to two thousand sleeping drunks.

Bill Shenker's split-log meat counter had survived the fire. They piled the sides of beef across it as quietly as they could. The Indians, who had followed them to camp, watched in silence but with broad grins lighting their dark faces.

"Around back of the tent now," Smoky said in a low voice. "We'll load out the important things first and leave the tent. Ask your Indian friends if they'd like to have it."

"I already tried to pay them for all the help they been," said Honker, "but they just laughed at me and said what good is money in the mountains."

"A foine big tent with only a few holes in it is different, I'm sure," said Smoky. "Tell them it's theirs if they'll help us load—only do be quite silent about it. I've a feeling our good will may not survive the unfriendly light of day."

Honker pulled around behind the tent. Smoky was already emptying the battery jars, which he sent the Indians to rinse out down at the creek. Beansie helped the Indians load the outfit on the wagon.

"Somehow I don't like the looks of things," Smoky murmured as he brought the cage of mice outside and set it down, preparing to open it and free the mice. "I've an instinct about such trouble, Honker, and no indeed— I do not like the looks of it."

"Just a couple of saddle bums," Honker grumbled. "Let's get out of here. Pay them no mind."

Two men, one burly and slab-faced, the other younger, gaunter, with a mouthful of bad teeth, had dismounted and were tying their horses to the scorched limb of a tree near where the Silverado had stood. They stopped for a moment to shake their heads unhappily at Bill Shenker's big safe. Then they came shambling toward the last remaining tent, separating as they came and walking ever farther apart.

Lou Burnside and Merle Watson had fled on foot just in time. They had no idea what had touched off the mob's wild rage, but their consciences were not exactly clear, and anyway no stranger lingers when he has running room ahead of a vengeance-crazed mob. Fortunately their horses ran in the same direction, and when they fled into the timber, they were soon able to recapture them.

All night they had squatted fearfully among the trees, watching the orgy of burning and destruction and wild drinking—especially the drinking. It was too bad for all that whisky to be wasted, but nothing that they could do about it occurred to either. They had ridden into the camp as softly as possible that morning, cold, tired, again hungry, and in the worst possible humor.

And the first person they saw was Honker Cahoon, the man who had humiliated them without bothering to lay his hand on his gun, down there on the Nevada trail. This time Lou Burnside did nothing to damp down his partner's competitive fire. In the first place, in the desolation of the ruined camp, they had nothing to lose by trouble now. In the second, Burnside's own touchy pride had been hurt.

As for Honker, he had been so busy that he had forgotten his past sins entirely. Probably better than anyone else, he knew how urgent it was to get out of camp before the mob got over its gigantic gang-drunk. He who had run from so many minor crises was not likely to offend his own devout cowardliness in a big one.

He looked up and beheld doom marching toward him from two directions, Burnside on the left and Watson on the right. Everything might have been all right, and he could have beat a rapid retreat into the timber, had not Beansie's voice suddenly sounded softly in his ear.

"You take the fat one on the left," Beansie whispered tremblingly, "and I'll take the mean little one, Watson. And let them draw first, Mr. Cahoon. We'll show these farmers a thing or two."

Honker, by one of the tricks the complex human mind does so easily, slid instantly into character as The Old Gunnie. Perhaps the beating of his own heart helped; perhaps the sudden twanging of his own banjo-string nerves pushed him over the edge of something or other. He was sitting on his heels, snapping the last padlock on their armor-plate money box, having added to their previous take the receipts of yesterday. In his mind was the figure $20,084, which represented the two-day income from the world's only electric mouse roulette game.

"Oh pshaw, don't you go getting no rediculous idees, boy!" he snarled. "A boy of only fourteen trying to let on that you're a riffraff fast-draw artist—why, you ort to have your pants whupped! You go help that off-lead horse of Smoky's. He's stepped over his tug again."

"Don't be a fool, Mr. Cahoon!" said Beansie. "They got us between them. They'll kill you sure as blazes. Let me have one. Merle Watson never seen the day he could draw with me."

As his temper went out of control, Honker shot to his feet, his scar leaping out as vividly as Smoky's artificial lightning flashes. But for the first time in his life he did not go deaf. He was like an actor who has lived a part so long that he has become the very character he had assumed on the stage. In full possession of his senses—if any —Honker Cahoon at that moment actually believed he was The Old Gunnie.

He said wrathfully, "Do as you're told, boy, or I'll take a strap to you! I been responsible for you, and I ain't going to have you mixing in with no common trashy no-good worthless hangdog yella-bellied riffraff fast-draw smart alecks! I declare, these two has gone too far this time. They have got to have their lesson, and I want you to get out of a grown man's way and—"

"Cahoon!" Burnside said stridently. "I'm calling your bluff, you old bluffer. Go for your gun!"

"Watson," Beansie almost screamed in a shrill boy's voice that betrayed him at the wrong moment, "you're all mine. Go for your gun any time. I'm ready!"

"Why you fresh brat, who you talking to? I got a good mind to take you up on that," Watson giggled.

"I wouldn't advise that, Watson," said a strange voice.

All four looked around. They could not help it. There stood a tall, well-dressed man in a flat-crowned hat, whittling carelessly at a soft pine stick.

Beansie made a strangled, choking sound. "You stay out of this now, dad-blame it!" he said. "You got no right to butt into another man's fight, and you know it."

"I'm not butting in," the tall man said wearily, "but I think these two farmer boys ought to know that you're the son of Worried Smith and faster than he ever was at his best. Faster than anybody I ever seen! But I tell you, Junior: If you get in a gun fight with these two, and you kill anybody, I'm going to warm your pants until you'll eat standing up for a month."

Lou Burnside made a sort of hiccuping sound. "You—you—you're Worried Smith?" he managed to say.

"That's right. And this is my cub. Danged no-good little whelp, he's gun-crazy—and look at the size of him! Did you ever see a fourteen-year-old kid with hands like that? It's no good trying to tell the little whelp anything. He has to find out for himself, and the trouble with that is, he's too good. My sins have catched up with me in my old age, and that rotten little brat of mine is prob'ly the fastest gunman that ever lived—at fourteen!" Worried Smith said mournfully.

A moment of silence. Then: "I don't believe it!" said Merle Watson.

"I do!" said Honker. "Everybody let me handle this little scrub. You take that gun off, kid, or dang me if I don't wear the belt of it out on your hind end. You hear me? Beansie—I said *take that gun off!*"

"No! I got a right to live my own life," Beansie snarled. And this time his voice did not break. This time it was the man's voice in him.

Honker started toward him. "Beansie, I'm through arguing with you. I'm going to whup your dad-blamed pants for you, that's what I'm going to do. Ain't I told you about all the riffraff gunmen I knowed in my time? Ain't I *told* you and *told* you that this scum is nothing but a lot of scum? What do you want to do, turn out as worthless as that worthless Watson tribe?"

"I heard that!" Merle Watson said in his nervous, giggling voice. "You can't talk about the Watsons thataway. Draw your weapon, Cahoon."

"Oh, you shut your dumb mouth, you—"

Too late The Old Gunnie saw that he had baited one of the most vicious gunmen in the world into a fast-draw contest. Too late he saw that he was not really The Old Gunnie at all. He was only cowardly old Honker Cahoon, the most craven man in the world, and the biggest liar.

But somehow his gun was in his hand, and Merle Watson's gun was in his hand. And somehow Honker heard his gun go off, and Merle Watson's gun went flying away into the mud, and there stood the most terrible of all the terrible Watsons, wringing his deadly right hand with his left and staring at Honker with his mouth open and all his bad teeth showing.

"Risky business, Cahoon," Worried Smith said. "Any time a man draws on you, you're a fool if you don't kill him. Shoot the gun out of his hand? Not I!"

"Well, you ain't me," Honker said, replacing his gun in its holster. He looked at Burnside. "Take your ninny friend and get out of here, you ninny! What are you waiting for?"

"Nothing," said Burnside. "Don't shoot, Cahoon. We're leaving! Just give us a chance."

Honker turned his back on them scornfully and marched into the empty tent, where Smoky O'Neill stood with his hands hanging limply at his side, his eyes big as saucers. Smoky got his arms up just in time as Honker pitched forward into them in a dead faint.

A man emerged from the timber to hail their wagon as they turned a curve a few miles south of the ruins of Camp Corinth. It was Bill Shenker, puffing at a cigar. "What's happening back yander in camp?" he said.

Honker and Blythe, sitting high on the tail gate of the loaded wagon, ignored him. Honker carried Beansie's

.30-30. Blythe was traveling light except for his unsatiated thirst, which gave him the shakes now and then.

"Them as is able are broiling your beef—burning it, rather," said Smoky O'Neill. "By evening they'll be trailing down the mountain. We owe you for the beef, by the way."

"You don't owe me nothing," Bill said wearily. "I ain't going to be a millionaire nohow. I'm so discouraged, if I was a woman I'd just set down and weep."

"Get aboard and ride along with us."

"And leave my safe behind? I reckon not!"

"But what will you do, Mr. Shenker?" Smoky asked.

"I got my bull wagon and a little camp back in the timber that nobody ever knowed about. A man can never tell when he'll need a hidey. When they're all gone I'll go up and take my money out of the safe and go home."

"To your ranch? There could be a foot of snow on the ground by then."

"I walked in, and there was two feet then. What become of that long, limber kid that was with Honker?"

"Went back with his daddy."

"Worried Smith. It sure was a famous gathering—Smith and Lou Burnside and Merle Watson and Honker Cahoon—yes, and before that, Dewey Score. I'll have some wonderful memories of Camp Corinth, all of 'em bad."

Smoky spoke to the broncs, and the wagon moved on. Bill Shenker vanished into the forest. Honker clambered over the load on the wagon and sat down beside Smoky.

"See here, we're going to have this out, Smoky. You roped me into a crooked game, like Worried Smith said. He wouldn't even let his kid take his share of the money, because it was crooked."

"Honker," said Smoky with a sorrowful smile, "all

gambling is dishonest, because it's based on man's greed to win without working what he cannot earn by work."

"That's just dodging the question. I want the truth, Smoky. Is mouse roulette a crooked game?"

"You saw all there was to see, Honker, me friend. Tell me this: How would I bribe a mouse?"

Honker remained unconvinced, but he gave up for the time being. Soon he took the lines and let Smoky curl up in a blanket on top of the load, to sleep. Honker missed Beansie, and that was the size of it.

Life, he saw now, was just one crisis after another. Here he was The Old Gunnie, one of the most famous men in the world, and he was not enjoying it one bit. He tried to remember the golden moment when he had outdrawn Merle Watson, recklessly and disdainfully shooting the gun out of the deadly kid's hand instead of drilling him. It was impossible to separate what had really happened from all the experiences that had never happened.

They made a lonely camp late that night, with Honker standing guard with both the .30-30 and his .45. They made an early start and still had not seen any of the refugees from the burned-out camp.

But two days later, far down the mountain, they caught up with two very tired and very hungry walking men. No one on the wagon recognized the two proprietors of the hard-rock mine, because none had ever seen them before. The two ex-magnates had let their horses escape the first night and had been afoot and hungry ever since.

They gratefully accepted a ride on the wagon. There was a pot of cold beans and the remains of two fried rabbits, which the luckless pilgrims accepted in tearful gratitude. The younger of the two then squatted in the middle of the wagon and tried to sleep.

On the seat Maynard and the Irishman were chatting away, fourteen to the dozen. Smoky was glad to have someone to talk to after two days with the taciturn Honker and the thirstily miserable Blythe.

"My word, electric mouse roulette, what a fascinating concept!" Maynard was saying when Jimmy began to listen consciously. "Do you mean to say it works?"

"Like a charm!" said Smoky. "'Twas good for ten thousand a day while it lasted. But I see one thing now. It should be a moving game—a couple of days here, three or four there. I believe people would quickly lose interest in it if it stayed past its welcome."

"Lose patience with it, you mean," said Honker from the rear of the wagon. "We're lucky we're not swinging from a tree limb back there, Smoky."

"Nonsense! But it still should be a move-about game, and now me wife will niver let me out of her sight. Me longest holiday in twenty-two years of marriage, sir."

"Why not lease your game out on a percentage basis?" said Maynard.

"Oh, I suppose we'd do it if we could find the right man. It takes imagination, nerve, coolness, a quick head with figures, and about ten thousand dollars that me pardner and me would want as an earnest payment."

"Jimmy and I would be just the men for it. One thing, however, worries me. What if someone hit us for a big pot before we had been in business long enough to pile up a reserve? Many a profitable game has been wrecked that way, you know."

"I know." Smoky glanced uneasily back at Honker. "It couldn't happen with electric mouse roulette."

Maynard said: "It can happen in any game. I once saw a woman who had never played dice before make eight straight passes. That kind of streak could break anybody."

Smoky puffed out his cheeks, thought it over, and let the air out explosively. "Not with electric mouse roulette. There's a bit of a device called an electromagnet, which I've no time to explain now. It's a scientific marvel, ye see, which few understand. Now when ye run the electric mouse game, ye lean with your hands on the table, in plain sight, while the mousie runs from hole to hole—see?"

"I see. That's what puzzles me—how you—"

"During this time," Smoky cut in, "yez make yer calculations on which hole yez can afford for him to go into. Pick one that leaves yez a comfortable profit margin for the scamper—say five hundred per cent—yet gives the crowd some winners too. Then press the right button with the tip of a finger under the edge of the table. They look like no more than tack heads; yet each closes a circuit activating an electromagnet that opens the trap under the proper hole. 'Tis the only one mousie can go into then, don't ye see?"

"I heard that!" came a honking, braying voice from the rear of the wagon. "I told you it was crooked!"

Honker stood up and picked his precarious way across the teetering load. Both men on the seat turned to face him.

"My word, a gold-studded gun!" Maynard exclaimed. "What do those glittering baubles signify, may I ask?"

"I don't know! I got this gun in a pawnshop in El Paso, and they was already on it," said Honker. "Now you listen to me, Smoky: I told you you couldn't fool me. This is a crooked game, and I don't want nothing more to do with it."

"'Tis not crooked but scientific. There's a vast difference, Honker, and it's merely coincidence that the difference is in our favor. Do sit down while the gentleman and I negotiate," said Smoky.

"I'm sure my partner and I can make money for ourselves as well as you, and thirty per cent doesn't seem at all out of line," Maynard was saying.

"There's also the ten thousand dollars in advance," Smoky reminded him gently.

"Reasonable, too," said Maynard. "We'll want to overhaul your outfit—something with more class—and we'll have a few thousand for expenses, besides."

Jimmy heard his partner blathering away as though they still had all that money. "You dummy, did you forget we was stuck up? We're flat broke, remember?" he said.

"Oh, Jimmy, you surely don't think I'm simple enough to ride down the road with our case money in a valise, hanging from my saddle horn! I've got it stitched into my clothes in various places. Stop complaining, and come here and learn how to run a game of electric mouse roulette."

In the back of the wagon Honker said, "You had it figured out from the first, didn't you, Perfessor?"

"Sure! The electromagnet is no mystery to me."

"How much did you win by it?"

"Nearly four thousand altogether. You're not angry, are you, Honker?"

"No. Perfessor, Smoky's going to make me rich whether I like it or not."

"I rather fancy he will, and me too, because I'll follow

the game wherever your new licensees go with it. I'll become a sort of silent partner, betting the safest numbers at the last moment before the lightning crackles. The one that will cost the house the least!"

"It's a sinful world, Perfessor."

"Right! We'll be sinfully rich."

"Nothing to do but enjoy it then."

The Old Gunnie relaxed. His swarthy face took on its characteristic look of ineradicable gloom. The wagon creaked on down the mountain, taking him and his gold-studded gun to a life of fame and riches in which truth would always be stranger than fiction. In time he might get used to it.

Wayne Collis